BODY TRAFFIC

Rita Y. Toews

BODY TRAFFIC

DOUBLE DRAGON

CHAPTER ONE

Sonja, Late May

Brakes squealed in protest as the old truck shuddered to a halt. Sealed in the cramped smuggler's hole surrounded by packing crates in the back of the vehicle, Sonja Sepsik crouched on a folded blanket. Fear squeezed the air from her lungs and fed her growing claustrophobia. Fists clenched tight, she fought the tremors of rising panic that flowed through her body. I'll be okay, I'll be okay, she repeated to herself as she fought the urge to beat on the sides of the compartment.

Above the wheeze and cough of the truck engine, Sonja heard the muffled voices of the driver and border guards as they haggled over the bribe required to allow the vehicle into Hungary without inspection. Bowing her dark head, she made the sign of the cross and whispered a quick plea for protection. Hospody pomozhy menee. God help me. While she didn't consider herself religious, she instinctively turned to her orthodox upbringing as a source of comfort in an effort to fight back her panic.

Although the words were unclear, the tone of the conversation outside sounded friendly. Smoke from a harsh European cigarette crept through the rotting canvas sides of the truck, worming its way into her hiding spot where it mingled with the dust and backwash of diesel fumes. She longed for fresh air. How long would it take? As the minutes ticked by, she forced herself to take deeper breaths and her body tremors eased.

A burst of coarse laughter punctuated a statement. The negotiations must be going well. Fjodor was right, she thought. In his last letter from Hungary her brother had assured Sonja that the arrangements to smuggle her out of Ukraine were secure. He also boasted that he had friends in the right places. People who would take care of everything. She closed her thoughts to the part of her conscience that whispered he would enmesh her in his world, a world she suspected flirted with illegality.

Shortly after his twentieth birthday, in 1988, Fjodor had slipped away from their home in Ushgorod to seek a new life in Hungary. He'd left only a terse note of farewell. Although devastated by the loss of the last male in the household, her mother hadn't seemed surprised by his departure. The middle child of three, Fjodor was the one who never really wanted to grow up.

One evening just before he left, Sonja's mother had pleaded with him as they sat around the table over their evening meal. "Fjodor, you must realize that to get ahead in life you need to settle down, get a good job and make something of yourself. Perhaps if you started to attend church again""

Sonja sensed her brother's rising anger at the veiled criticism in her mother's comment. He'd interrupted her; his tone harsh. "My dear mother. You assume that if we put enough effort into life it will reward us. But in truth, life is a game we play with fate. Where did hard work and decent principles get our father? And your perfect son, Misha, the one who made something of himself?" he asked with ill-disguised contempt. In the stricken silence he provided his own answer. "He joined the army to serve his country. But where is he now, Mother? No. Life isn't about hard work, it's about connections."

Shoving his chair back from the table, and leaving his food uneaten, he'd made his way to the door. "It's about who you know," had been his parting shot before he walked out and slammed the door.

Fjodor's farewell note had disappeared into the deep pocket of one of her mother's identical black dresses, never to be seen again. She'd sought comfort in her great faith. She believed in miracles. She'd prayed earnestly that her husband would suddenly walk through the door, alive and well; that Misha would return from the void into which those "missing in action' in Afghanistan had disappeared; and that Fjodor would find his place in life and return from Hungary a wealthy man.

While Sonja was still a young girl her mother had dragged her to prayers at the Ushgorod Cathedral. The prayers themselves held no meaning for her but the sonorous chants, the richly carved dim interior glowing with mellow candlelight, the thick smell of incense rising from the censers, together with the drone of the prayers, had given the church a mysterious quality, a feeling of safety. The sense of peace her mother felt while she prayed in the cathedral had also flowed into young Sonja. Did God really hear those prayers her mother sent upwards with such fervour? Sonja had seen little evidence of His answers in her life. The Almighty Creator of all things would be far too busy to hear the pleas of a worn out old woman sitting in a shabby church pew.

As she grew older, Sonja refused to attend church regularly, although she attended faithfully at Christmas and Easter, hoping to recapture that sense of peace. Now in her fear she prayed, Hospody pomozhy menee.

Finally the slam of the truck door and a cheerful call of farewell signalled the end of the negotiations with the guards. With a sigh of relief, Sonja allowed her tense body to relax. It was foolish to give in to fear. Fjodor surely knew what he was doing. The bribe would have been sufficient, and if the guards were too diligent it would just cause them more work. Uncovering an illegal entry meant a lot of paper work, a lot of investigation and a drop in revenue. The guards had learned long ago that the best policy was ignorance.

The stress and the heat in the truck box had taken their toll on Sonja. As the vehicle set out once again on its journey to freedom, the hum of tires and swaying motion combined to lull her to the brink of sleep. Drowsily, she gave herself over to dreams of her new life with her brother in the paradise of Hungary. She felt no ties to her old life . . . a life that had held little joy .

She remembered nothing of Kiev, the capital of Ukraine, where she was born. Soon after her birth her father's employer had transferred them to the smaller town of Ushgorod. As Ukraine was part of the Soviet Union at that time, she and her two older brothers were Soviet citizens, and grew up in the regimentation of communist life.

At a young age, Sonja learned there were many subjects that were taboo in her home. One was the disappearance of their father just after he'd spoken out in favour of the Czech Republic's attempt to "give socialism a human face.' When Fjodor turned his back on his spartan life in Ukraine and slipped over the border to Hungary, Sonja and her mother never discussed his reasons for leaving. Years of sorrow and heartache were walled up behind the old woman's silence. Perhaps she feared that if ever she allowed even a trickle of sorrow to escape she would be washed away in the flood that was sure to follow.

After completing high school, Sonja became a finisher at the local furniture plant. When not focussed on lamenting the scarcity of shoes, or long working hours, the conversation in the cramped company lunchroom often centred on black-market goods smuggled across the border from the golden land of Hungary. The deprived citizens of Ushgorod were quite familiar with the superior standard of living on the other side of the border; even barbed wire couldn't contain that kind of news. Money made in the smuggling business more than made up for the danger involved.

"Peter's brother, Karl, smuggled in twenty pairs of pantyhose and got ten times what he paid for them!" Tatania, the young woman who worked next to Sonja on the finishing line, often bragged about her boyfriend's adventurous brother. A sweet person, Tatania expected very little from life other than the hope that one day Peter would make their living arrangements legal and assumed Sonja's ambitions were similar to hers.

"Has he any left for sale?" Sonja asked half-heartedly, as she bit into her black bread and salami sandwich. It seemed unlikely that an item as scarce as pantyhose would remain unsold for long, but one could always hope.

"Sorry. They were gone in an hour. But if you want some you could let him know. He keeps a list of items people want. And as beautiful as you are Sonja, all you would have to do is smile and he would go out of his way to get it."

Swallowing the dry wad of heavy bread along with her disappointment, Sonja replied, "Well why didn't he bring in more if he has customers already lined up?"

"Because he doesn't have a license for more, silly goose."

"License? What do you mean, license?"

"Ah, Sonja. You're such a naive girl! The customs officers issue licenses for smuggling only a certain amount of contraband goods. Then they take their cut of the profit. If smuggling gets out of hand they'll be replaced with new customs officers who are less greedy. It's to their advantage to keep the amount that comes in to a minimum, so they issue licenses."

"What a mess," Sonja said with a shake of her head. She finished the sandwich but it hadn't satisfied her hunger, a hunger food would never be able to satisfy. The barren lunch room, the grimy factory, the shabby apartment she shared with several roommates since the death of her mother, all added up to a soul numbing existence that fuelled her growing dissatisfaction. She understood how Fjodor must have felt before he left. She too felt

10

trapped in an environment devoid of anything but the bare necessities of life. She wanted so much more.

Occasionally, Tatania brought a hard-to-come-by fashion magazine to work. As they flipped through the well-thumbed pages together, Tatania would tell Sonja that her features rivalled those of the women on the glossy pages. Her dark, arching eyebrows framed large eyes whose colour changed with the light, sometimes hazel but more often a pure green. When she was younger she had often yearned for a creamier Russian complexion, but as she matured she'd come to realize that many considered her dusky skin tone and high cheekbones exotic.

While others envied her beauty, Sonja found her looks a liability. In the factory she wore her long auburn hair tied up in a knot under a kerchief but she could do little to disguise her softly curving figure or attractive features. Without family or a husband to protect her, she was vulnerable. Within months of her mother's death, the factory scheduler had approached her just after lunch.

"Sonja, I've made changes to the line assignments. You'll be added to the finishing line tomorrow."

Her first reaction was shock, then defiance. "You can't do this to me, Erik. I'm not strong enough to handle the finished products. Women have been crippled trying to move those heavy pieces to the crating line." She drew herself up and squared her shoulders. Perhaps a bluff would work. "I'll lodge a protest if you force me on that line."

11

He circled her slowly, openly admiring her hair, the line of her throat, visually measuring the length of her legs enclosed in baggy coveralls. A smile tugged at the corner of his mouth; the fox had cornered his prey. "And who would you bring your protest to, my lovely Sonja? Superintendent Rostov?" His eyes mocked her now. "His only interest is his bottle of vodka. Of course, we could perhaps reach an agreement, you and I. Would you care to join me for supper tonight? We can discuss it. I've been known to change my mind." He traced her jawbone with his index finger.

Her skin crawled at his touch and his words caused a sick feeling to wash over her. He was right. No one would listen to her complaint and she didn't have the option of quitting. She lasted four days on the finishing line, then lost her virginity and much of her self-respect to the scheduler.

She no longer had control over her own life. The only way out of Erik's grip was to ally herself with someone who had more power than he. But that was Superintendent Rostov, and the thought of sharing his bed held even less appeal. In an unforgiving world, Sonja soon learned that her female assets were her only assets. I will hold my head up, no matter what I'm forced to do, she thought fiercely. Her tears of shame fell less often, and then not at all.

The close proximity of Hungary and the good life she was sure her brother had established for himself were powerful lures. She spoke basic Hungarian, but not enough to bluff her way out of a one-on-one encounter with a border guard if she tried to cross and got stopped. To be caught at the door of Paradise and then turned back . . . no, she refused to imagine it.

Her mother had been dead for over a year before Fjodor received the news and finally contacted her. This time her tears had been tears of relief.

The rear door gave a metallic shriek as it opened and the noise drew Sonja from her dreams. Fresh air and narrow beams of light found their way into the murky darkness of the truck box as invisible hands began to unload the cargo that sealed off her hiding spot. Was her brother on the other side, or would she be taken to another meeting place? Nervously, she ran her fingers through her tangled hair and made an attempt to smooth the wrinkles from her dusty clothes. With the backpack that held her only possessions clutched in her hand, she squared her shoulders to meet her future.

As the cargo wall was breached full sun flooded in, momentarily blinding her. The figure of a man appeared, silhouetted against the harsh light. As her eyes adjusted to the glare, she took in his features, tall, thin, too thin really. His clothes, while not labourer's clothes, hung shapelessly from knobby shoulders and narrow hips. Brown hair with a hint of curl crowned a face with a familiar dark complexion and hazel eyes. She caught her breath at the sight of an ugly scar that began just below his ear and ran along the ridge of his jaw, ending at a point beneath narrow lips that were now stretched in a grin of welcome.

"Fjodor?" she whispered nervously. Was this the prosperous brother she'd hoped to meet?

With a slight shake of his head her brother replied: "My name is Ferenc Sebes now, Sonja. It's a good Hungarian name and we're in Hungary."

Another explanation edged its way into Sonja's mind" Fjodor Sepsik was on the run from someone. She had an unhappy feeling that her mother's prayers had not been answered.

CHAPTER TWO

Stan Boyko

As the plane banked left for its final descent into Winnipeg International Airport, the passenger in seat 21C strained to get a view of his hometown. Laid out beneath him in neat geometric patterns, the predominantly French speaking area of St. Boniface was easily identified by the beautiful edifice of the old St. Boniface cathedral that had been destroyed by fire in 1968. Using the edifice as a landmark he located the replacement structure.

A stream of tiny figures flowed from the entrance. A wedding perhaps, or a funeral. Unbidden, the memory of his father's funeral came to mind; there had been a few old men in attendance, plus a nurse from the personal care home where he had spent his last few months. His gaze lingered too long on the cathedral and the landscape below slid from his view before he could pinpoint the house that had been his family's home.

It's eight years since I've been back, Stan Boyko reflected, and it looks the same. Viewing it from above, he realized again just how small the city actually was. In its heyday Winnipeg had been known as the "gateway to the West.' Today, it paled in comparison to its upstart younger sisters, Calgary, Edmonton and Vancouver, which had all experienced building booms.

The 767 slowed to a halt at the gate and the engine sounds died away. He was home, or at least the closest to any place he could call home. Stan joined the crush of passengers as they retrieved their items from the overhead bins. Of necessity he was traveling light, so after locating his coat and small duffel bag he made his way into the terminal, by-passed the mass of people around the luggage carousel and left the terminal. Stepping into the warm June sunshine, he hailed a taxi.

On the ride downtown Stan mentally reviewed his cover story. Life would definitely be a lot simpler in Winnipeg than it had been when he worked the waterfront in Vancouver. He had traveled undercover from Vancouver to Winnipeg using the alias Dimitri Bolenko, but that was to be the last time Dimitri traveled in style. From now on he'd be a Ukrainian seaman who had jumped ship in Halifax several years ago and was slowly working his way west. He felt he could work with the cover; he had worked with a lot less in the past.

"You say you want to be dropped in Chinatown, eh?" The taxi driver's voice broke his thoughts. "Near the gate?"

"Sure, that'll do."

"Must 'a been a short trip."

The lack of luggage. The driver was observant. "No, actually I've been away for a couple of years. My things are being shipped later this week." The lie would do for someone he'd never see again anyway.

"Welcome back. You haven't missed much. Nothing changes in Winnipeg."

It's true, Stan thought. You go away, things happen to you and you change, but then you come back and it's like you've stepped into a time warp.

Rae and Jerry's Restaurant still occupied its corner on Portage Avenue. The Greyhound buses still lumbered out of the depot across from The Hudson Bay store on Colony Street, hydraulic brakes hissing, engines spewing diesel fumes. Then, just before the cab made a left turn at Smith Street, he noted that the windows of what used to be the Eaton's store were covered over in brown paper. Large bolt holes marked the spot where the proud name had once hung above the building's huge brass doors. Then again, maybe some things do change.

The sight of the building brought back memories of his mother so strongly that he smelled her perfume in the musty confines of the cab. He saw her again, a vibrant woman, smiling with pleasure as she left the house to meet her friends for their monthly get-together at the restaurant in this same Eaton's store. Lunch and shopping, every month like clockwork until the first stroke robbed her of that simple pleasure and so much more. Her death several months later stole the joy from his father's life and marked the start of his slow decline into senility.

The cab pulled up in the shadow of the spectacular Dynasty Building that dominated Winnipeg's Chinatown and formed the northern border of the city's old Exchange District. Stan paid the driver and took a few minutes to stroll the quiet pathways of the building's water garden. It was a powerful reminder of Vancouver's Chinatown and he realized he'd miss the west coast city. Enough of this. It's time I start earning my pay.

He crossed the street to enter a low, nondescript building that served as the satellite office for the undercover unit of the Intelligence Services of the Royal Canadian Mounted Police.

The telephone call earlier in the month informing him of his transfer from the Pacific Region of the RCMP to the North West Region of Criminal Intelligence Services in Winnipeg, had come as a relief. For three years Stan had worked as an undercover narcotics officer on the Vancouver waterfront without a problem, but in the last couple of months he'd grown suspicious that his cover was about to be blown. Too many questions were asked, too many sideways looks thrown his way. There wasn't much he could put his finger on, but after ten years in the business, he'd learned not to discount gut instinct, especially when accompanied by the sensation of something boring into his back. It was time to get out, and he'd made the call to arrange his transfer from the docks.

Within days, after a very public argument with the shop steward, he was informed that his services at Burrard Shipping were no longer required and he'd received his final pay.

Stan's face was too familiar on Vancouver's waterfront, the major entry point for narcotics smuggled into British Columbia and a tight community. He needed to be moved from Vancouver, and the border crossing into the US was too close to the port city to be a viable alternative.

There hadn't been much to say good-bye to when he packed up his belongings. The undercover business didn't lend itself to close relationships, and if his landlady gave him a smile when he left, it was no doubt because he'd paid his rent in full and didn't try to stiff her for the final month by hauling up stakes in the middle of the night. His last act before heading to the airport, and a trip into a new life, had been a stroll along the sea wall in Stanley Park for a final look at the ocean he had grown to love.

Stan didn't protest his assignment to Winnipeg. Having grown up there, he knew his personal knowledge would be an asset. He didn't anticipate moving in the social circles he once had, so he felt reasonably sure of not running into any old school acquaintances.

The satellite office was located in a nondescript limestone building fronting on Princess Street. The wood door opened silently on well-oiled hinges.

"Good afternoon sir, may I help you?"

"Dimitri Bolenko to see Inspector Willis. I believe he's expecting me." The alias slid smoothly off Stan's tongue as he set down his duffel bag and fished in his inner coat pocket for the wallet containing his new Manitoba driver's license.

The plainclothes officer on duty took more than a casual glance at the id, comparing the photo and personal information with the man who stood in front of him" male in his late twenties; dark brown eyes; medium height, slim but with strong hands; a deeply tanned long firm face. The years of manual labour on the docks had broadened Stan's shoulders and added sun-bleached streaks to his overly long dark hair. He stood, patient during the careful examination, confident that his appearance would stand up to the even more critical scrutiny of the streets.

Apparently satisfied with what he saw, the officer returned his id. "Right. The Inspector is waiting for you. Said to show you in when you arrived." He led Stan down the hallway to the office of Inspector Mark Willis, his contact at Criminal Intelligence Services Manitoba, known locally as CISM.

He entered a standard federal office, one that could be found anywhere in Canada. In an attempt to add personality to the room, someone had hung several Inuit art prints on one wall. Beige carpet, a few bilious green filing cabinets, a desk and two chairs completed the decor. From a west window, afternoon sunlight bathed the room. A big man rose from behind the desk and moved to greet Stan. He was just past the prime of life. Years at a desk job had softened muscle and gravity had taken care of the rest. His handshake, however, was firm, and the look in his grey eyes was direct.

"I'm Inspector Willis. It's a pleasure to meet you, Constable Boyko. Please, have a seat." He smiled, pointing to one of two well-worn chairs drawn up to the desk. Then, rather than return to the more comfortable seat he had just vacated, he picked up the file lying on the desk and settled himself in the second chair. "I've just read the latest annual report on organized crime. It's gratifying to see that thanks to the RCMP, we've been able to put a substantial dent in the narcotics trade along the Pacific Rim this year."

Settling into his chair, Stan exhaled loudly, and nodded. "Yeah, I read it too when I did my sign out at "E' division. I won't go so far as to say they're being overly optimistic, but unfortunately trying to curb the narcotics trade is rather like trying to plug a leaky dike. You get one hole stopped up and another starts leaking."

"Hmm," Willis grunted in acknowledgement. "A feeling shared by all enforcement units. Well, . . . on a more personal note, "no problems with pulling out of Vancouver?"

"No, it seemed to go smoothly. They did a good job getting me out fast so there wouldn't be much damage control needed." He drew his eyebrows together in a slight frown. It nagged at him that he couldn't figure out why his cover had started to unravel. Until he could pinpoint what it was, he was likely to make the same mistake again, a mistake that could be deadly next time.

Inspector Willis leaned back in his chair and linked his hands behind his head. "So . . . tell me. Have you been able to keep abreast of what's been happening here in Winnipeg over the last few years?"

"Nothing other than what I've read in the papers, or seen on television. I haven't had ties with anyone here for quite a while. I've heard some pretty negative press that brands Winnipeg the murder capital, and lately the arson capital, of Canada, but I take that with a grain of salt. It could be just press-talk, and highly overblown."

"Not by much I'm afraid. Winnipeg's a small city and it's close to the us border. That makes it tempting for organized crime."

Stan nodded. Organized crime groups preferred to target smaller cities for their illegal business, finding it easier to establish a legal business as a front for money laundering, or even drug trafficking. Still, he had a hard time equating Winnipeg, located in the southern Manitoba Bible belt, with criminal elements.

21

Willis continued, "Now we've got the biker problem to add to the mix. It has the potential to become pretty nasty. Lately, the Hell's Angels have tried to branch out so there's been some jostling for position with our own biker factions and the Indian Posse gang members. Everyone wants to be in position for a larger piece of the pie if the Angels are successful."

He reached for a piece of paper on the desk and handed it to Stan. It was an excerpt from the latest CSIC report:

"Eastern European based organized crime groups

EEOC in Canada are well connected to criminal counterparts

in Russia, Europe and the United States and function

as integral parts of large-scale international organized

crime networks. EEOC is increasing its involvement in

drug trafficking in some regions . . .

The Hell's Angels are one of the most powerful and

well-structured criminal organizations in Canada. In

1998, they formed two new chapters: one in British

Columbia and one in Saskatchewan, for a national total of

16 chapters. The establishment of a chapter in Ontario

remains an objective for the group."

Stan raised his eyebrows in surprise, "This states the Angels are targeting Ontario. Do they want to move into Manitoba as well?" If Manitoba was also being targeted, it was very bad news indeed for the province.

"Ontario may be too tough a nut to crack right now, but whatever the reason I'm afraid there've been some definite feelers put out here. And, if our intelligence is accurate, we've got an even bigger problem because the word is out that the European crime network is using the rivalry of the biker factions to their own advantage. You know how it goes; stir it up, and while they're at each other's throats, you walk in and scoop up the goodies."

He leaned forward to review the file in his hands. Stan noted that it was his personnel folder.

Willis leafed through a few pages then brought his gaze up to meet Stan's. "Anyway, here's where you come into the picture. I understand from your dossier that you're fluent in both French and Ukrainian?"

"Yes, sir," Stan nodded. "My mother was French. I grew up in St. Boniface and went to a French language school there. My father, on the other hand, was Ukrainian and insisted that I learn that language as well."

Concern clouded Willis' eyes. "Winnipeg's got a huge Ukrainian community. Do you have a lot of relatives here?"

Stan shook his head. "None. But as a kid I'd spend most of my summers with dad's relatives in Saskatchewan and they spoke only Ukrainian at home. I've occasionally found need for both on the docks, so I've been able to keep them up fairly well."

"Good. You'll definitely have use for Ukrainian, and odds are you'll need your French as well. You'll be working undercover, and we want to minimize the possibility you could be recognized. You'll have to cultivate a Ukrainian accent." With a slight smile the Deputy Commissioner added, "How do you feel about a moustache?"

Stan grinned as he ran his hand over his neatly shaved upper lip and chin. "Until two weeks ago this mug hadn't seen the light of day for three years. I'll start working today on getting the moustache back."

"You'll work under a loose agreement from CISC. Your goal will be to infiltrate the local crime ring that operates in concert with the Ukrainian mafia out of Europe. I stress the word loose because CISC seems to be playing its cards very close to its chest on this one. Although they're out to destroy, or at least cripple, the European based criminal organization, and say that they welcome any intelligence and investigative reports from the RCMP, they've given us virtually no feedback.

"Also, we seem to be in the unfortunate, though not unfamiliar, situation where there hasn't been much cooperation from the local police force either. Just recently they've started refusing to submit forensic specimens to the Central Forensic Laboratory in Ottawa, claiming that the new lab here in Winnipeg is fully equipped to do the job." He slowly tapped his front teeth with the fingers of his steepled hands. "I must admit, it hits a raw nerve with me, Boyko. We've heard rumblings of corruption at that new lab."

Rivalry between competing police forces wasn't anything new. The recently opened federal lab in Winnipeg would give the local policing agency a way out of submitting any specimens to the RCMP lab, as they'd been required to do in the past. By using the Winnipeg lab, they could control access to the testing results. Whether they chose to share any information that came their way on a case within their own jurisdiction was strictly up to them.

Stan had always worked hard to establish a good working relationship with local authorities and the effort had usually paid off. Few were reluctant to share information with him. Willis' comment about corruption in the lab, however, disturbed him. If any of the personnel at the lab had been corrupted, evidence sent for testing could be manipulated and would be useless in a court of law. What an incredible coup for criminals, having a police lab with the capability of doing DNA testing in their back pockets!

Shocked, Stan asked, "Do they send all evidence to the lab here, or just certain tests?"

"A good three-quarters are being dealt with here. Others are still being sent to Ottawa. But the ones that we're most interested in are being tested here; the ones that are most likely to be related to high profile crime such as the European crime ring and the biker rivalries. I suspect it's a way for the police to remind the RCMP that this is their city and they have the ability to deal with their crime, however big. Of course, if the rumours about the lab are true . . ." He let the thought hang there in the air, heavy with implications.

The possibilities for abuse were many, but two immediately came to Stan's mind: altered DNA results and human organ trafficking. Rousing himself from his thoughts, he addressed the older man. "So, as I see it, there are three areas that I'll need to get into: the activities of the Ukrainian mafia, their involvement with the biker gangs, and the corruption of the federal lab. Is there any hard evidence of actual dealings between the mafia and the bikers?"

"Nothing concrete, of course. There have been a few visitors to town from the us and from Eastern Europe who have shown up in biker locales. We've run them through the computer but they always come up clean. No surprise there. A fellow named Sinclair runs a lot of the establishments where the bikers tend to congregate: bars, strip joints, massage parlours, escort services, that sort of thing. He's also had some dealings with a couple of Ukrainians on our watch list. He's got his hand into any thing that makes money, including at least one transportation company and an insurance company."

"Have you told the local police chief that an undercover RCMP officer will be looking into the European mafia and biker connection?"

Willis shook his head. "Unfortunately, we don't think it would do your investigation any good to get his back up over your presence. He's made it well known that he feels he's on top of the situation here and that he's the one who will be collecting the laurels when Winnipeg is cleaned up. I'm afraid you're being asked to go deep cover, and that's a pretty lonely place to be. If you tangle with the law because of the company you keep, a brawl, whatever, then you're Dimitri Bolenko and you're on your own. If things go really sour and you need to be pulled out, the RCMP will take the responsibility, and of course," he tapped the cover of Stan's file. "Your orders will be posted in your personnel file.

"I've got a telephone number here that you can use for contacting the cover team we've set up, and there's a safe house if you need it. You'll need to memorize the phone number and the address. I've got a package of material that lists the details ready for you to review in an office down the hall. You can take as much time as you need to go over it. Now, any questions you can think of at this point?"

The sunlight that had found its way into the room was beginning to lose its intensity, throwing softer shadows. Outside, the traffic noise had lessened as rush hour wound down. The telephones in the reception area were now silent; the day was winding to a close.

Stan shook his head as he rose from the chair and collected his bag. "Not really. Maybe I'll have a few after I've gone over the information you have for me. Any chance there's some cash in that package?"

"Yes." Willis allowed himself a rueful chuckle as he too rose and moved with Stan towards the door, "Not much, I'm afraid. Wouldn't do to have Dimitri too flush with cash. He seems to have fallen on hard times."

With his hand on the door Stan turned, "Oh yes, one more question. Am I cleared for a gun?"

"Sorry, Stan. In the places you'll be hanging out it's common practice to be frisked before you're allowed to enter. If you're packing a gun, you're more likely to be singled out. If the situation warrants it, the cover team can back you up and they'll be armed."

Stan nodded and left the Inspector's office. He liked the man and his feeling was reinforced a few minutes later when a carafe of hot coffee was delivered to the room where he sat reviewing background material. He spent the next hour looking at papers on the European mafia, the bikers and the new lab. Then, he pocketed the used bus ticket from Thunder Bay and worked the major portion of the money from the envelope into the shoulder pad of his coat; a few small bills went into the worn pockets of his jeans. Well, Dimitri, welcome to Winnipeg, he thought as he made his way out a side door of the building and headed toward Main Street and the Harbour Light soup kitchen. At the thought of food, his stomach reminded him that lunch was just a memory.

The area of the city around Main and Logan stood in sharp contrast to the more prosperous business district of Winnipeg. Wealthy middle-aged entrepreneurs looking for a trendy address were slowly bringing several of the crumbling buildings in the Exchange District, designated as heritage buildings, back to life as loft apartments. But on the fringe area of the district the story was quite different. Here, buildings were boarded up or bore defaced "For Sale' signs, evidence of their long tenure on the market. Here, the seamier side of the city began to show its face; pawnshops, used furniture stores, tattoo parlours and junk stores, disguised as "antique' stores, abounded.

Traffic was light and Dimitri jaywalked across the street to enter the mouth of an alley that backed on the soup kitchen. A thin crowd was gathered a few paces into the alley but it soon became apparent that food wasn't the attraction. Shouting, cursing and blunt thumps of body blows attested to a fight in progress. Dimitri joined the ring of onlookers.

This wasn't a contest of equals, but rather a one-sided affair in which a burly individual was laying a systematic beating on a slim man with Oriental features. The underdog did his best to ward off the blows but he was no match for his attacker. Somewhere near Dimitri a man murmured to his female neighbour, "Someone sure wants to send a message."

"Yah! I heard he tried to expand his business into biker turf!" The statement was punctuated by a high-pitched giggle ending in a damp snort. As Dimitri watched, the girl raised a grubby hand to her nose to wipe away the thin line of blood oozing from her damaged nasal passages. When she realized she had an audience, she lost interest in the fight and turned her attention on the stranger in the crowd.

"How do you know it's the bikers laying a licking on him?" Dimitri challenged her.

"What? You stupid or something. Tattoos . . . black leathers. Or maybe it's the Harley over there that gives it away . . . duh!" She slapped the heel of her hand into the middle of her forehead and crossed her eyes, to the delight of several onlookers.

"Well, maybe the guy just doesn't like Orientals," Dimitri countered. The beating wound down and the thug stooped to wipe his bloody right hand on the shirt of the barely conscious man on the dirty pavement.

"Nah! I know the pipsqueak. He's been running some girls and selling a little coke on the side. That's biker territory, man, and you don't mess with bikers."

The wail of a police siren interrupted the conversation. A cruiser squealed to the curb and two patrolmen exited the car, putting their hats on as they approached the wary crowd. The car had barely come to a halt when the rev of the Harley filled the alley as it shot to the opposite end and made a sharp left to disappear down the street. Bits of trash and discarded paper fluttered in its wake.

The huskier of the two police officers bent to examine the inert figure on the ground while the other singled out a few witnesses, then tried to get the rest moving.

"All right, all right show's over. Get a move on it, people. Come on! Show's over I said . . . beat it!"

A hand gripped Dimitri's arm roughly and shoved him. "Get a move on, now!"

Staggering back, he turned, instinctively wanting to protest the rough treatment by the cop. But training controlled his personal indignation, and he followed the group back to the sidewalk. Grumbling amongst themselves, they headed, en masse, to the soup kitchen.

It was a mild evening and he'd soon have at least a hot meal, if not a nourishing one. Not bad when compared with his first post up north at Great

Slave Lake. Up there winter was seven months long and being on patrol hadn't been fun. In the north he'd been up against the hostility of nature, here in the city he was up against the hostility of man. He had come to realize that of the two, the latter was the more dangerous.

CHAPTER THREE

Anel Blondeau

The muted ping of an elevator alerted Laurence O'Connor that someone was about to arrive on the second floor of the Federal Central Laboratory.

Damn! Who the hell comes to work at seven o'clock on a Monday morning?

He killed the lights in the accounting office and positioned himself behind the slightly opened door. He had hoped to have a good hour to bring his own set of books up to date before staff began to arrive. Some might call it foolhardy to keep his personal accounting in a public place, but he agreed with the maxim that the best place to hide a book was in a library. The lab handled a lot of police forensic work so the personnel were conditioned to confidentiality and locked files.

As director of the lab, he had every right to be in the file room, but it wasn't a common place to find him, and he didn't feel up to making an excuse this early in the morning. With any luck at all, the early riser would go straight to the kitchen area and make a pot of coffee, giving him time to relock the filing cabinets and get his records back to his own office.

Bright overhead lights sprang to life and brought the common area of the room into sharp focus. The sound of high heels rang loudly on the tile floor. A woman. As she passed across his line of vision, he was glad he had taken the precaution of

32

not being seen. The early bird was Anel Blondeau. He followed her progress down a spacious aisle to the locker area. He had a few minutes while she hung up her jacket and retrieved a clean lab coat from the never-ending stack in the cupboard.

He eased the door of the file room open a little wider to allow more light to spill in and quickly closed up the files he had been examining. Within seconds the folders were back in their appropriate places, and he had gathered his papers from the top of the cabinets. He gave silent thanks for his decision not to make photocopies this morning. He would have never heard the arrival of the elevator over the sound of the copier.

Anel emerged from the locker room, a lab coat draped over her arm. He watched as she made her way toward the kitchen, but she paused in the centre of the open work area and turned in a slow circle, as though admiring her surroundings. The facility was new and the lockers, sinks, tables, chrome chairs, glass and instruments all gleamed brightly in the artificial light. The complex equipment and tiered shelving dwarfed the woman, accentuating her vulnerability. It was this fragile quality that had attracted him to her the first time she had stepped into his classroom two years earlier, while he was still teaching at the University.

Although he wouldn't call her a beauty, she was still an attractive woman. Her petite build and wavy chestnut hair were classic French features inherited from her mother; a Swedish grandmother had contributed a fresh complexion and strong cheekbones. They were a good match with her firm nose and chin. How many times had he gazed into

33

her hazel eyes to seek the flecks of gold there? One of these days his patience would pay off and he'd do than look, but it had better be soon. She was proving far less pliable than he'd hoped. Even the recent deaths of her parents hadn't broken her enough to turn to him for comfort. He'd applied a lot of pressure to get her hired at the lab and he didn't care to think it was wasted effort.

Anel surveyed the room then drew a deep breath, savouring the faint smell of newness that still lingered in the air. She'd been alone in the facility before, but this morning it felt a little unnerving, so much so that she shivered. She shrugged on her lab coat and made her way to the coffee room. She'd had a restless night; that probably accounted for her sense of unease.

The weekend had been tedious. She'd spent the entire two days alone, as usual. Until recently she was able to keep herself busy enough on weekends with make-work projects, and didn't mind her self-imposed isolation. But lately it had begun to matter more. I think I'm ready to come back into the world of the living, she thought. But the world of the living would now be a lonely, empty place. As empty as this lab.

She drew fresh water and poured it into the coffee maker, all the while battling a vague anxiety. It wasn't even 7:30, the work day in the lab didn't start until 8:30. What had possessed her to come in so early? The machine began to gurgle and hiss then released a stream of pungent coffee into the glass carafe. She turned her attention to the discarded magazines strewn across the table.

"Is that fresh coffee I smell?"

The words were spoken at her elbow and she reacted instinctively. With a gasp she turned and raised both fists, ready to confront her attacker. The next moment strong hands clamped on her wrists and held her tightly.

"Hey, sorry I scared you. Are you okay?"

It was Laury O'Connor, the lab director and her former university professor.

As the adrenalin faded away she felt weak and almost collapsed into his arms, drawing back at the last moment.

A mist clouded her vision, then cleared. "Sorry. I-I over reacted. I don't like people sneaking up on me like that." Trembling, she ran her fingers through her hair and straightened her lab coat. What a rotten way to start the day. The coffee machine gave a final gurgle, then fell silent.

"Well, I came in for a cup of coffee and almost ended up with you in my arms." His tone was light, an obvious effort to calm her. He reached to straighten an errant curl of her chin length hair.

While Laury prepared his coffee they chatted, but it was hard for Anel to concentrate fully on the conversation. Despite the strong attraction she felt for him, her guard always came up when she was in his company. He seemed to sense her tension this morning and finally turned to leave, then paused at the door. "I'm expecting a delivery this morning but I'll be out of the office for most of the day. Would you please go down and sign for it?"

She forced a smile and nodded. Once he was gone she found it easier to relax and get over the fright.

Monday mornings were usually very busy, and this Monday was no exception. Anel soon lost herself in her work. At nine o'clock the phone at her elbow rang.

"Anel," the specimen-receiving clerk said, "there's a delivery here for Dr. O'Connor. Someone needs to sign for it."

"I'll come down and sign it myself," she answered and replaced the instrument in its cradle. This would be the delivery he was expecting.

Choosing the stairs over the elevator, Anel made her way down to the receiving area. The call about the delivery brought back memories of her fright this morning. Why hadn't she allowed herself to cling to him rather than draw away?

Six months ago she had been stunned when her former professor and mentor suggested she apply for a position in the new Federal Central Laboratory. The previous summer Anel had been fortunate enough to get a term position as lab assistant to the well-known biochemist. A first-class student, she was quick to pick up the skill of DNA preparation and analysis. No doubt her experience in that summer employment, minimal as it was, had played a part in the Professor's suggestion that she apply for the position.

Locked in her grief, she had ignored the invitation. But Laury had followed up by actually delivering the application form and a glowing reference letter. Within a month she'd received a telephone call requesting she come for an interview, and a week later another call advised her that the position of supervisor in the analysis department was hers. The job, Anel reflected, had been the first good thing to happen to her in several years.

At the receiving dock, the package had been x-rayed and was waiting for her. She signed for the Styrofoam cooler labelled "Urgent, Attention of Dr. L. O'Connor," thanked the clerk, and decided the weight of the cooler warranted using the elevator for the return trip. Back on the second floor, she entered the delivery into the log book as number 1167, specimen for research. Invariably this type of parcel contained research organs for the experiments Laury was conducting. Suitable organs for transplant were in great demand throughout Canada and the United States, but supply was short. Such scarce organs would never be made available for a research lab. On the other hand, research quality livers, kidneys and bone marrow, although not abundant, occasionally did become available and would arrive for Laury from the teaching hospitals. She put the cooler in the specimen fridge and left a note on Laury's desk to say that it had arrived and was logged in.

"Time for a break!" Roger, one of the junior lab techs, called as he passed her office.

Where has the morning gone? she thought as she acknowledged the invitation and laid aside her work on a police sample. The case, a particularly savage attack on a man by his neighbour, had made the headlines several days earlier. What emotions, what depths of passion would cause a man to turn on another man? Anger? Jealousy? Maybe even hate? Dark emotions, all of them, and usually kept buried deep inside, a passive energy waiting to be set free. What impulse released them? Fear would,

37

she reflected. She had experienced that this morning. Her impulse had been to strike out, no matter the consequences.

When she thought back to the incident in the coffee room, she was embarrassed by her reaction. Laury must think her a complete idiot. It wasn't the first time she had reacted so violently when surprised from behind.

She shook her head to dispel the gloomy thoughts and made a slight adjustment to the test calibrator before she rose from the bench. It was a real coup for the lab to get police cases, and Laury had asked that she personally do the demanding tests required on this sample. She arched her back to relieve her tired muscles, then massaged the nape of her neck. It would be good to relax and chat a bit with her co-workers over coffee. She was feeling far too introspective this morning.

The yeasty smell of warm cinnamon buns and the pungent aroma of coffee greeted her as she entered the room where a small group of employees were gathered.

"Hi, Anel," Lisa called in greeting. The insistent beeping of the microwave signalled the buns were warm. With a quick stab of a finger, tipped with a magenta nail, her co-worker popped the appliance door open and removed the fragrant rolls with a theatrical flourish. Everything Lisa did was accompanied with a touch of drama.

"You're just in time for cinnamon buns a la Lisa," she said gaily as she deposited the treats in the middle of the table. "Voila! Maybe this will help put some meat on those bones of yours. Obviously your own cooking isn't doing the job."

"Now, now," Roger chided. "Not everybody can be as voluptuous as you, Lisa. You wouldn't happen to have a bit of butter for these little goodies, would you?" he asked, as he deftly scooped the largest roll from the pile.

Anel watched with a smile. Monday morning was her favourite time of the week; a relief from the gloom of lonely weekends. She enjoyed both her job and her colleagues.

Paul, one of the techs, was thumbing through the scrapbook on the coffee table. Someone with foresight had collected news articles and clippings covering the history of the lab since the initial announcement by the government several years earlier. Now, the collection was secured in the pages of a neatly bound book.

"Can you believe this kind of facility was ever built in Winnipeg?" he queried as he turned the pages, careful to avoid smearing sticky cinnamon bun syrup on them. "When the rumours started circling that a class four lab would be built in one of the provinces, I'd never have put my money on Manitoba's getting it."

Although she had seen all the clippings before, Anel joined the group peering at the photos and articles as the pages were turned. She, too, was surprised that the three levels of government had agreed to finance a research laboratory in Winnipeg. A lab of this level would give local police agencies the option of using its services for forensic work, rather than using the Central Forensic Laboratory in Ottawa.

The Federal Government had made another surprise decision, and allowed the University of

Manitoba's medical faculty, along with the provincial College of Physicians and Surgeons, to name the new director of the facility. Their decision was unanimous. The directorship was awarded to Dr. Laurence O'Connor, a relatively young research scientist and professor at the university whose name was known for his research in DNA.

The next page of the scrapbook revealed the familiar features of the new director. His magnetism fairly leapt from the photograph. The black and white photograph was the perfect medium to accentuate the strong lines of his elegant face and the square white teeth that flashed from a mouth that smiled, even in repose. Somehow, the viewer knew the eyes looking out from the photo would be grey, the eyebrows a shade darker than the hair that fell to meet them. White wings of hair just visible at his temples gave Laury O'Connor's handsome face the look of maturity, a useful attribute for one running the newly founded lab. Here was a man the public would love to love; a man who could stand as an equal with the head of the Centres for Disease Control and Prevention in Atlanta.

Anel had sat with the other 150 staff members of the lab in the first few rows of Centennial Concert Hall for the official opening ceremony. Sadly, there was no one in the crowd to share her exhilaration; two months earlier her parents had died in a small plane crash while enroute to a nursing station in northern Manitoba.

Unbidden, the memories welled up, her father's strange silences and her mother's anxious demeanour just before they left for the north. Why hadn't they treated her like an adult? Why was the family lawyer, as executor of her father's will, the one to tell her that Dr. Claude Blondeau, the well-loved family physician, was a victim of the Bre-Ex Mine financial scandal? The news of his losses in Bre-Ex explained much: the sudden sale of the family home and her father's decision to take on the extra duties of the nursing station, even though he shared a thriving medical practice in St. Boniface.

Her parents were her only family, and had been her only support system. Without them she felt as though she was lost in a thick fog with no coordinates to show her a way to escape.

The thump of the heavy scrapbook as it was flipped shut on the coffee table interrupted her thoughts.

"Thanks for the treat, Lisa," she said as she rose to rinse her hands at the sink.

"Bienvenue," Lisa replied in her stumbling French. A self-conscious giggle brought out the dimple in the young woman's rounded cheek. Lisa often lamented the fact that the employees of the new facility were required to be bilingual since the Lab was officially a Federal building. "You're so lucky you already speak French, Anel. It's really hard to learn a second language! And where are we supposed to practice it? My family's all Ukrainian, for Pete's sake! Were you raised French?"

"I sure was," Anel replied to the question. "As a matter of fact, my mother liked to tell the story of how Grandfather Labossiere would only allow her to marry if my father promised to keep French as the language spoken at home."

She had many fond memories of her childhood home in St. Boniface, a small French community on the southern side of the City of Winnipeg. It was a world unto its own. Well-kept homes and ornately designed religious institutions pressed tightly against stylish shops where French was spoken.

"Then how did you learn to speak such perfect English, if you were raised in such a pure French household?" Pamela, another lab tech, cut in. Pamela was one of the lab employees who openly resented the bilingual edict. She also seemed unhappy that someone as young as Anel had been given a senior position in the lab. Her tone was abrupt, a good match for the sharp features that gave her face a feral look. The light atmosphere in the coffee area evaporated.

"Well," Anel responded, with some caution, "I grew up wanting to be a doctor, like my father, so I knew I would have to speak English. That meant attending a high school outside St. Boniface. The sisters at St Mary's made sure I became a fluent bilingual Canadian," she concluded, hoping to put an end to the touchy conversation.

Repeating her thanks to Lisa, Anel left the coffee room to return to her office. Unfortunately, Pamela's expression of animosity towards her had dampened her spirits. Intuition told her that Pamela would make a formidable enemy if she felt crossed.

CHAPTER FOUR

Budapest

Seated with her brother at a patio table of an expensive cafe along the Danube promenade, Sonja attempted to set aside her misery and submerse herself in her surroundings. The day was mild, and on the breath of the faint breeze that caressed her face she caught the scent of roses.

A spectacular panorama claimed her attention on the opposite shore of the Danube. The Royal Palace on the crown of the hill dominated the scene. From this distance, the neo-gothic cathedral of King Matthias, with its tiled multicoloured rooflines, appeared to be a gingerbread confection. And the neighbouring Fishermen's Bastion surely was fashioned from white lace rather than stone! A fairy tale city for a young woman deprived of beauty. The breath-taking view was in sharp contrast to her mood.

The past two weeks had been devastating. Hungary was not the "paradise' she had expected, for she found little happiness in her new circumstances.

She had spent her first week of freedom in a flurry of excited shopping sprees and sightseeing. But either Ferenc or one of his friends had escorted her around the fashionable shops making suggestions for replacing her meagre wardrobe, or pointing out the highlights of the city. The men made her edgy. Their conversation often too familiar. Finally, after a particularly obnoxious suggestion, she refused to go on further escorted outings, preferring to venture out on her own. Finally, the whispers of her conscience, whispers she had chosen to ignore while still in Ukraine, could no longer be set aside.

Yesterday, she had been out for a walk in a nearby park when she spied her brother with someone near a small grove of trees. As she approached to say hello, she saw Ferenc hand the man a packet in exchange for a large wad of money. As he slipped the money into his jacket pocket, he had exposed a gun in the waistband of his pants.

"Feri," she asked softly, as she extended a hand across the table to gently touch his sleeve. "Why do you carry a gun?"

Sonja's question ignited her brother's suppressed anger. For the past week he had been moody, alternating between agitation and sullenness. At times he never stopped moving, tapping his feet, cracking his knuckles, pacing restlessly. Now, he thrust his half eaten lunch aside and reached for yet another cigarette from the pack in his pocket. Ferenc seemed to exist on cigarettes and little else.

"That's none of your business, Sonja! What gives you the right to question what I do? You've been nothing but a pain in the ass since I brought you here!" He made no effort to control his voice and diners at other tables turned their heads to stare at the couple.

His angry reply stung, and tears filled her eyes. Sonja hung her head to hide her shame. "Please,

Ferenc, people are staring. Why are you so angry with me all the time? What have I done?"

"It's not what you've done, it's what you won't do! And please, don't play dumb with me!" He leaned closer and lowered his voice, but the intensity still lashed at her. "Sipos has about had enough of you. You're too choosy, or maybe you're just stupid. What were you expecting when we brought you here, Sonja? Do you think he put up the money for your trip out of the goodness of his heart?"

Sonja was stunned. "Your boss paid the money to bring me out of Ukraine?" The realization that Sipos Sandor and not Ferenc had paid for her trip to Hungary sickened her. Sipos was nothing more than a thug and he treated her brother like dirt under his nails.

"Do you think I have the kind of money that bribe took? He put up a lot of money for you and you're expected to pay it back. All he's asking is that you appear in a couple of movies, do a little acting. Who knows? You may even enjoy it."

Her surroundings receded in a grey mist and a roar filled her ears. He wants me to be a whore! My brother is trying to pimp me! As she struggled with the dreadful thought, little things stood out in sharp clarity. A small piece of lettuce hung on a thin tine of her fork. The man at the next table had dust on the bottom of his pant leg. How could she just disappear so the conversation couldn't happen? Her throat was tight and she swallowed painfully. She forced her words through numb lips.

"There are other ways to earn money, Feri. I can cook, or work in a factory. I can work as a cleaning woman""

"Peanuts, Sonja! You'd earn peanuts. I need to pay Sipos back and I need a lot of money coming in all the time. I have . . . debts to pay. I need to make real money! You and me, we could make some real money, Sonja. I'd look after you, protect you. You've grown into a really beautiful woman. But first we have to get Sipos off my back." Exasperated, he lashed out at her, his tone harsh. "What the hell did you expect?"

"There . . . there's got to be another way! I won't sell myself for you or for anyone else! I'll find some other kind of work! I'll . . ."

"You just don't get it, do you, Sonja? You don't own your body any more. It belongs to Sipos Sandor until we pay him back!" In his fury he ground out the butt of his cigarette with such force the filter crumbled in the ashtray.

From a terrace opposite the restaurant the pounding rhythm of a jazz-band matched the wild beating of her heart. First Erik, the scheduler, and now her brother and Sipos, she was nothing more than warm flesh to be used, or sold.

A man entered the patio from the direction of Vaci utca, the Fifth Avenue of Budapest. Well-heeled tourists could spend more in an hour on Vaci utca than she earned in an entire month of backbreaking labour at the furniture factory. Ferenc also spotted the man and followed his path toward their table. He hissed at his sister, "Just keep your mouth shut and smile!"

Another blow. This outing, suggested by her brother, was actually a prearranged meeting with his boss.

Although Sipos Sandor's background was Gypsy, he could easily be mistaken for a Latino. His black hair lay slicked flat to his head forming a shiny cap, and a thin black moustache traced a dark line above his full lips. His eyes, however, shattered the illusion of languid elegance" they were the hungry black eyes of a predator.

He arrived at their table and reached with a manicured hand to draw a chair back from the table. Sonja caught a glimpse of the enormous signet ring on his finger. The ring bore a large stone with an engraved family crest, purportedly a sign of his noble lineage. Everything about him was perfect, so perfect he must be a fake. Nevertheless, as he sat down at the table, a waiter with sense enough to sniff the odour of a big tip appeared instantly at his side.

"What can I serve you, sir?"

"I'll have a cognac, Courvoisier."

Sipos Sandor was not a large man, but the power of his presence made him seem to take up more space than he actually occupied. Turning his full attention on Ferenc and Sonja, he addressed them in a silky voice. "Hello, Feri, and greetings my dear, Sonja. I hear tales about you, my pretty one. You're not happy with your employment?"

Gathering her courage, Sonja shot back, "I'm not a piece of meat to be passed around, or posed in the nude behind glass, like a mannequin, to excite men!"

His demeanour remained calm but a fire glinted in his black eyes. "And tell me Sonja, what did you expect?" The question was rhetorical; he expected no answer and Sonja remained mute. His tone became menacing, fairly dripping with venom as he continued. "I have no patience for ungrateful employees, and I'm sure Feri can tell you what happens to anyone who gets on the wrong side of my good humour."

Her brother's fingers flew to the long scar on his cheek. Ferenc had refused to discuss the source of the scar with Sonja. Watching his subservient attitude with Sipos, she now felt certain that Sipos had inflicted the wound that caused it.

"No!" The desperate plea broke from Ferenc's tight lips. "She just needs a little more time, Sipos. She'll come around."

The waiter returned to the table so the little group fell silent as he placed the drink before Sipos on a small serviette. Sipos paid the man and waved away the change from a large bill. A man and woman at the nearest table departed, leaving them alone on their corner of the patio.

Ferenc sat white-faced, gripping the arms of his chair with tense hands. Sipos leaned closer. He extended his finger as though pointing a gun and spoke softly. "When I want to hear your voice, Ferenc, I'll ask you to speak." Settling back into his chair, he stretched his elegant legs to their full length in front of him and took a sip of his cognac. "Aah," he exhaled. "A drink to be savoured in fine company." Replacing the glass on the table, he linked his fingers across his stomach and sighed in contentment, the picture of a man enjoying the company of friends.

"But, you know, Sonja, I'm a reasonable man. Just ask your brother. If one of my employees is unhappy with our working arrangement, I do my best to find a solution that suits both of us. In your case, my dear," he said with a nod of his head in her direction, "I have a proposal for you."

Sonja swallowed hard, her throat so dry it produced an audible click. He toyed with her, challenged her to beg. She remained silent, but her mind screamed the question he wanted her to ask. What?

The silence grew between them. Sipos raised an eyebrow as though seeing her with new respect, and flashed a smile that actually made it to his dark eyes. "Well . . . I may have made a bad bargain. However . . . I have a business relationship with a woman from Canada who's here recruiting girls for several businesses she owns there. It seems Canadian men like European girls. Naturally, they have to be good-looking, pleasing, willing and healthy. I'll allow her to discharge your debt to me if she finds you attractive enough."

Sonja held no illusions as to what the business arrangement was. She would be sold into prostitution in Canada. She was worth more to him as a sale than she would be if he disfigured her or had her killed outright for defying him. Panic seized her and his words faded into the background, only half heard.

Maybe she should give in and do what they wanted. No, she couldn't live with herself if she did that. She hadn't left Ukraine to become a prostitute.

Time was what she needed. Time to think of a way out of this nightmare. She turned her attention back to what Sipos was saying.

"You'll have a legitimate contract for a year, a work permit and an entry visa if she finds you suitable. Feri," he extended a small business card to her brother. "Have her at the Hilton tomorrow at 10 o'clock. Show them this card at the desk; they'll give you the room number." He dropped another bill on the table as he left. "Have a drink on me."

The minute Sipos' turned his back Ferenc dug his cigarettes from his pocket and lit one with trembling hands. "Jesus, Sonja, do you know how lucky you are?" He held the card as he read out loud: "Rosa Sinclair, Theatre Manager, Winnipeg, Manitoba, Canada. Hmm, Manitoba, Canada . . . that sounds familiar. I think we have an uncle living in Canada. And Manitoba sounds familiar. Oh well," he said with a shrug of his narrow shoulders. "Canada's a big place and who knows where he is, or even if he's alive."

Sonja sat numbly, still trying to absorb her sudden change of fate.

In response to Ferenc's knock, Rosa Sinclair opened the door to an elegant two-room suite at the Hilton. Sonja's impression of the Canadian was that she had been quite pretty at one time, but at some point over the years she had stopped caring how she looked. She was a large woman, yet traces of her faded beauty were still visible around her mouth and the curve of her cheek.

Greeting Sonja and Ferenc in broken but passable Ukrainian, Rosa led them to a sofa fronting an expansive window. Once they were all

50

comfortably seated, she turned her attention to Sonja.

"Has Mr. Sandor explained the arrangements to you, my dear?" As she spoke Sonja saw Rosa's eyes pass over her body, appraising her hair, her face, her breasts. "I've agreed to pay your debt to him, and in turn, he has released you to me. Now, if we can agree on your expenses, I would be willing to give you employment in Canada."

"Expenses?" Sonja blurted. "You mean I would work for you, yet I would owe you?"

"I hope, my dear, that you are not so naive that you don't understand a business arrangement." She began to list expenses on her fingers: "Your airfare, your upkeep, your work permit, your medical insurance in Canada . . . that will run into thousands of dollars. They are legitimate business expenses, you must understand that."

"And I'm to be responsible for all that?" The amount would be staggering; maybe enough to keep her in Rosa Sinclair's debt for years.

"Who else?" the older woman asked in feigned surprise. "I have to compensate Sipos for his generous assistance with a new passport for you before you can even travel. Since you don't speak English, once you're in Canada I can't start you in an escort service where the big money is, so I'll have to employ you as my housekeeper until you pick up enough English to work in a massage parlour." She paused to arrange herself more comfortably on her overstuffed chair. As she did so the nylon stockings encasing her plump legs hissed, like aroused snakes. She continued. "Your initial debt to me will be 5,000 Canadian dollars, but you should be able to pay that back to me in a year."

The rapid sentences in accented Hungarian were hard to follow. Sonja turned to Ferenc, desperately seeking some input from him, but he refused to meet her eyes, choosing to stare at the plush nap of the carpet. He was lost in one of his periodic fogs. His gaunt face had a greyish pallor, and with one hand he listlessly picked at the ragged cuticles of the other. She would get no guidance from him.

Clutching herself in a desperate hug, Sonja rose from the sofa and wandered to the window. Outside, the grey morning had turned even darker. Heavy drops of rain smacked against the window adding to the chill she felt deep within. She would have to make her own decision; the brother she had known was dead to her.

Rapidly she reviewed her choices. If she stayed here and acceded to Sipos, sooner or later she would share Ferenc's fate. Although she had no proof, she was sure he was an addict and dependent on Sipos for his supply of drugs. If she continued to defy Sipos, he would maim or kill her as an example to any who might follow suit. If she went to Canada, there might be a chance to break free from Rosa Sinclair before she was put to work in a massage parlour or an escort service. She would have breathing room while she learned English.

"Where are the papers you want me to sign?" she asked as she turned from the window to face her new employer.

An hour later Sonja and Ferenc sat in the hotel bar.

"In five days I'll be in Canada, Ferenc. You said we had an uncle living there. What can you tell me about him?" If she had just one person she might be able to turn to . . .

"He was our mother's brother. I guess he was a lot younger than her and she practically raised him. Anyway, they were very close and she named me after him. That means his name would be Fjodor Podrinski. "He dug at an imaginary groove in the table with his thumb, his face set in a deep scowl. "He was involved in some scandal. We weren't supposed to talk about him, but Misha told me a couple of things. Let's see now . . . he fought with the Germans . . ."

From her chair across the small table, Sonja watched with sadness as her brother fought through his fog to remember anything that might help her.

"Oh, right! Misha overheard a quarrel. Father said our uncle was so stupid he would probably step in the same dung heap twice and that he would be the cause of the family's ruin. He came to the house one day with a parcel that he swore contained some sort of Nazi war treasure. He wanted father to hide the bundle until he could return for it, but Father turned him away, screaming something about not wanting to get involved with stolen Russian artifacts."

"Do you know for sure that he went to Canada?"

"I'm quite sure. Misha said he came back the next day to see mother. He told her he had found a way to get to Canada. I'm not sure if it was Manitoba, but I think it would be someplace where there was a large Ukrainian population. He said some day he'd be a rich man . . . Another family dreamer." The bitter sound of defeat was clear in his voice. It was the closest he had come to admitting that the fires of his dreams were now ashes.

Not me, Sonja vowed. I won't be just a failed dreamer.

CHAPTER FIVE

Winnipeg, Canada

The new specimen was a challenge, and Anel spent the entire morning on it. By noon she needed a break, and outside, golden rays of sunshine beckoned. Unfortunately, there were no pleasant parks or green areas close enough to the lab for a noon stroll. As she stood at the elevator, debating whether she should eat a sandwich in the staff cafeteria or bring it back to her desk, the elevator doors opened to reveal Laury O'Connor.

"Ah, Anel!" Laury exclaimed in apparent delight. "I was looking for a lunch companion and look who shows up. Please, join me. It's the perfect day for a salad at an outdoor table on Corydon. We can use the excuse that there's some lab business to go over, if you feel you need an excuse."

Since she was on her way to lunch anyway, she could think of no reason to refuse the offer. The sunshine looked very inviting, and so did Laury O'Connor.

With an expert touch Laury guided the Lexus through heavy noon hour traffic on Portage Avenue, then took a right onto Osborne. Anel settled into the air-conditioned comfort of the leather seats and studied her companion.

An avid golfer, Laury's handsome face was bronzed by the summer sun. The tan accentuated the tiny lines just beginning to form at the corners of his eyes. He exuded elegance and charisma, with a dash of charm thrown in for good measure. No wonder many of the girls in his university classes had been attracted to Professor O'Connor.

Unlike other female students, who would have eagerly spent a night in his bed in exchange for a better grade, Anel had kept her distance from him while she was in university. As though conscious of her decision, he seemed to seek her out. On more than one occasion, he had joined her at the cafeteria for a quick lunch, or "chanced' upon her taking a stroll during a break in classes. She told herself it was because she was a returning mature student, that he enjoyed spending time in her company. And although the role of coquette was not part of Anel's nature, she did find the companionship of the professor gratifying to her ego. She enjoyed his friendship, and opened up to him on more than one occasion, but she refused to allow their relationship to go any further.

It wasn't just Laury O'Connor that Anel held at a distance.

"Anel, why don't you date? You're going to end up a dried up old maid!" her friends teased one day when they witnessed her gentle rebuff of a fellow student who approached her for a date. "Open up to life a little more!"

Am I being silly? she asked herself. Am I a prude? She wrote it off as having been brought up in a sheltered home. She had been extremely shy as a young child and at times that shyness still prevailed. But she wasn't a child anymore, and she was astute enough to realize that the aversion she felt to anything with sexual overtones was definitely not natural.

She blushed in red-hot shame during anatomy classes when the male students covered up their own insecurities by teasing their female classmates. The usual reaction of the younger female students to explicitly sexual jokes was less awkward than hers. Although older than most of the other women in the class, Anel found the jokes almost unbearably embarrassing. The root of that unease was linked to an incident in her past. She had given the event a name, "the bad time,' in order to define it, but she refused to confront it.

It was summer, and Uncle Mark, her mother's brother, was visiting. Out of touch with the Blondeau family for years, he had unexpectedly resurfaced in Winnipeg when Anel was twelve years old. Uncle Mark was a strange man and neither her father nor her mother was particularly happy to have him around.

From their whispered conversations, Anel learned that as a teenager he had been a troublemaker and had left home after a scandal involving a girl. Try as she might, she couldn't remember when he left again that summer. She did remember being happy he was gone. The thought of him brought the memory of rough wood pressing against her back and the smell of cologne, but nothing more. A barrier went up in her mind preventing her from remembering the specifics of what had happened. But she knew. Oh yes, she knew very well what had happened. She lived each day with the knowledge, and the fallout.

She shook her head to clear her thoughts. Enough of this! She was tired of being lonely. It was time to put aside her grieving for both her family and her innocence and make a life for herself. If she couldn't get over it on her own, then perhaps she'd give in and go for therapy. Laury O'Connor had been patient with her the past year. He had given her a coveted summer position as his researcher, put her forward for her present job, and openly sought her company while at work. She was a fool to think he would wait around forever while she sorted out the demons messing with her psyche.

"Damn!" Laury braked hard to avoid rear-ending the vehicle in front of them. They were at confusion corner, a tricky intersection where several streets came together in a confusing tangle of traffic lanes. Unsure of which lane he should be in, the elderly driver of the other car had come to a full stop in the middle of the intersection. Laury cut to the right then turned onto Corydon, the main street of Winnipeg's Italian district.

Funky little cafes vied for attention on both sides of the tree-lined street. Several had set up patios on the sidewalk or in tiny courtyards. Parking was always a problem in the area so they cruised the cross streets until they found a spot, then walked back to the main thoroughfare.

Anel loved this unique part of the city. Loved the rich aroma of Italian food mingled with the smell of French fries doused in vinegar. She even loved the crowds. The sidewalks were jammed with strolling tourists and loitering teenagers out to enjoy the freedom of their summer holidays. The occasional local walked by with purposeful steps, gripping heavy shopping bags crammed with organic vegetables and high fibre bread. A small group of happy kids clutching brightly coloured cones streamed out of a gelati shop.

Laury steered her to the opposite side of the street so they could walk in the comfort of the shade. "Do you like clams, Anel? I know a restaurant here that serves delicious linguini with clams."

Clams. They weren't her favourite food, but he looked so enthusiastic. "That sounds delicious."

At Mama's, he requested a table on the patio, fronting the quieter side street. When the waitress offered menus, Laury waved them away and ordered the house specialty, linguini with clams, and two iced teas.

They settled back in their chairs to enjoy the warm caress of the summer sun. The tiny patio, lined with colourful planters overflowing with flowers, was the perfect spot to observe the ebb and flow of the street.

Laury broke the comfortable silence. "I'm surprised you accepted my invitation for lunch."

She laughed lightly at his pointed comment but couldn't quite bring herself to meet his eye. "Good grief, Laury. You make me sound like some kind of hermit!"

The waitress brought their iced tea and Anel toyed with the glass, rolling the coolness of it along the inside of her wrist. She felt his eyes on her, and the silence that had been so comfortable only moments before was now filled with tension. This is ridiculous, she chided herself as she focused her attention on the low wrought iron railing that separated the patio from the sidewalk. I find the man attractive, intelligent and charming. Maybe too charming, a voice inside her whispered. Nonsense. She brushed the thought aside. Suddenly, she felt his hand cover hers and she drew in her breath with a soft gasp.

"Anel, how many times have I asked you to lunch, or supper? I've invited you to the symphony and to the movies. You always seem to have an excuse. I'm quite encouraged that you actually accepted this lunch . . . Dare I call it a date?" One of his elegant eyebrows rose to meet the wayward shock of hair that fell over his forehead. He withdrew his hand but continued to hold her eyes with the force of his gaze. "Neither of us is a child, Anel. I'm sure you've realized by now that I find you very attractive and I'm trying to pursue a relationship with you."

He'd voiced what she had sensed for some time. One word from her would put an end to the relationship before it even began. The seconds lengthened. Fighting rising panic, she cast about for an answer. A familiar confusion flooded her thoughts, making it hard to concentrate on his words. Finally, she whispered, "Please, Laury, I need a little more time. I'm just getting over the loss of my parents and I'm feeling a little overwhelmed by my job . . ."

"Of course. I'm sorry I pushed you." Smiling, he once again took her hand and squeezed it gently in a protective gesture. "Let's enjoy our lunch. And speaking of lunch" here it is."

The waitress smiled at them as she deposited two plates of linguini alle vongole on the table. Anel felt sure that in the woman's eyes, they were a romantic duo out on an afternoon date.

***

Laury O'Connor found it difficult to keep his mind on the article in the Lancet. It featured organ rejection; a field he needed to keep abreast of, however his thoughts kept drifting to the lunch he had just shared with Anel. Was he wasting his time on her? He hoped not. Maybe he wasn't giving the lady enough credit. She might be just a shade too cautious, or too smart, to be easily manipulated.

The thought of the startled look on her face when he'd touched her hand brought a smile to his face. Yes, she seemed to be quite capable of resisting his charms and, if nothing else, that made the chase all the more appealing. He still had time to make up his mind, and if she didn't fit in with his plans . . . well, nothing would be lost but time. And he could feel her weakening.

He watched her through the glass window of his office as she removed another specimen from the fridge. If he could just gain her complete trust . . . oh, what a coup!

CHAPTER SIX

Monday afternoon, and the sky over the prairie was wall-to-wall blue. James Sinclair regarded the scene on the pool patio of his elegant Tuxedo district home and grunted in disgust. His wife, Rosa, reclined on a lounge chair near the pool in a curvaceous sprawl worthy of a Rubens painting. The effect was somewhat marred by the glass of lemonade, undoubtedly spiked with vodka, in her hand.

She's put on weight again; the trip to Europe must have been a success.

Her weight was one of a number of things about Rosa that disgusted him. Their marriage was on the rocks and she was rapidly becoming a liability.

He swirled the drink in his glass and regarded his own physique in the reflection of the patio door. A bit of a paunch, but what did one expect at 50? He was short and tempted to have his shoes fitted with lifts for an additional inch. So far he had resisted. His thinning brown hair and wide nose would have made him appear rather drab but for the large, good-humoured mouth that drew the viewer's eye.

He focused once again on the woman at the pool. She would have to be dealt with soon, before everything fell apart. He'd worked hard and had taken big risks to get where he was. Now, just when that elusive brass ring hung mere inches beyond his reach, it was in jeopardy because of her business, a sleazy enterprise that paled in comparison with the big bucks he could draw in. He stepped out of the house into the heat of the patio.

"Hello, Rosa. How did your trip to Budapest go?"

"Tiresome, as usual. I've been back a week and I'm still suffering jet lag." She didn't bother to rise and greet him, although she did push her sunglasses up to rest on her head. "Have you been out of town on business, or just spending time with one of your ladies?"

James refused to be baited and, ignoring the question, asked one of his own. "Did you bring anything interesting back?" It was sweltering on the patio, with barely a breath of breeze. The water looked inviting so he moved towards the pool house where a few bathing suits were kept.

"I signed up four girls, but only one has any real class. Unfortunately, she's Ukrainian and doesn't speak a word of English, so she'll have to stay here for a couple of months until she can pick up enough to carry on a decent conversation. I think she's worth the investment. She can do the housework, and who knows," she took a large gulp from the glass in her hand and flashed him a humourless smile, "you may find her interesting yourself."

She had managed to get under his skin and spoil his interest in a swim. James decided he might as well talk to her now, rather than later. He drew a patio chair into the shade of a large basswood tree and settled into it. "And the other three?" he asked, less out of interest than as a way to avoid what would surely be an unpleasant conversation.

"Passable English. I'll advertise them as "exotic,' and if that doesn't work, I can always put them in with Louisa's crew."

There! An opening. Leaning forward in his chair, James allowed his hands to dangle between his knees as he addressed her. "Rosa, I'll say this again. You've got to get out of low-end prostitution. You're getting the bikers riled up and it's not worth the hassle. They're getting more powerful. They've received an infusion of funds from one of the national biker groups and they're flexing their muscles. It's only a matter of time before they come after either you or some of your girls."

"Well, well." Rosa arched an eyebrow. "Are you concerned for your wife, my dear, or are you concerned for yourself?" She formed a moue with her generous lips and blew him a kiss before reaching for a bottle of suntan oil. The fronts of her legs had begun to redden, and she turned her attention to the task of slathering them with the dark liquid. "Actually, you're a little too late with the warning. One of my boys received a beating in Chinatown a couple of weeks ago. And Louisa's been warned that if any of the girls cross into biker territory they'll have their faces cut."

"Give up the street level stuff! Keep the massage parlours and escort service if you want. That doesn't compete with the bikers. They'll leave""

Rosa shot from her chair, sending the suntan oil flying across the patio where it came to rest against a row of potted flowers. The oily liquid splashed against one of the terracotta pots, staining the clay surface. It struck James that there was a lesson in the spreading stain, but he had no time to pin down what it was.

Rosa planted her hands firmly on her full hips. Her face was flushed and when she spoke, her voice vibrated with both anger and sarcasm. "I'm not a coward! I know if I give in once they'll push me further, and then further again, until I'm out of business. And please, stop with the "I'm worried about you' crap! You don't give a shit about me! It's your own business you're worried about. And I don't mean the bars and strip joints."

James sat, stunned by her words. What was she insinuating? He abandoned his chair and made a grab for one of her oily arms. It was too slick and she broke his grip easily, although faint red lines marked where his nails had gained some purchase on her skin. "What are you talking about?" he demanded as she spun away to put some distance between the two of them.

"Do you think I'm stupid? That I don't know what you're up to? If I step on someone's toes I know who I've crossed and what to expect. But you! You're walking in a minefield, lover boy, and you don't know what might be coming your way. Every law enforcement agency in Canada and the us is watching for just one small slip. Then, one of these days," Rosa made a flicking motion with her fingers. "Plink! the dominos start falling and guess""

"Shut up!" James bellowed. He seized a towel lying on the small table beside her lounge chair. The table and lemonade crashed to the patio, but he ignored the flying glass and began to daub at the beads of sweat that rimmed his hairline. He wiped the oil from his hand and, still in a rage, flung the towel at the object nearest at hand, a trellis heavy with honeysuckle vine. "Get in the house!"

Clutching her robe, Rosa reluctantly picked her way around the glass shards as she made her way to the patio door and entered the dim house. James followed close on her heels. Once inside, he grabbed her by a slippery elbow and steered her into a room converted into an office. Soundproof panelling ensured their conversation would stay private. With the door firmly shut, he turned on her again.

"Idiot! You're out there acting like a God damned fishwife! Everyone and their dog can hear you mouthing off about my private affairs. Things you know nothing about!"

"James, I may not be a rocket scientist, but I sure as hell do know what's going on! I know about your Dr. O'Connor and the lab. After a couple of your quiet little rendezvous with the man, I figured I'd better get informed and did a little investigating. I discovered a few things. My girls have ears you know. The good doctor is a bachelor, and he has a taste for brunettes."

A finger of ice-cold fear crept up his spine. His voice was tight when he spoke. "Rosa, it's dangerous to meddle in something that's none of your business."

"Oh, but I'm making it my business! I have access to this room and I saw the fax, James. The one that came from Ukraine about a certain pharmaceutical company in Switzerland that's under investigation by Swiss authorities." She played the innocent, widening her eyes and tapping her index

66

finger against a plump cheek. "What did it mention, now? Oh, yes! Human organs, that's right. Let me see, kidneys, bone marrow, pituitary glands, and that's just part of the menu. As I understand it, my dear, these products can command a very high price throughout the industrialized world." She laughed, a brittle, gay laugh that filled the room. "Too bad, isn't it, James, that they also cautioned that a "possible Canadian connection is suspected.' You'll have to be more careful, won't you?"

She wasn't bluffing. She'd figured it out and he'd be the one to answer for it. Perhaps, just perhaps, he could reason with her. "Rosa, I've always thought of you as a sensible woman. Please don't get involved in my business. Think of it this way: when you put your finger in a hornet's nest the sting doesn't stop at your finger tip. It can engulf your whole arm. It can even be deadly."

She appeared to be totally enjoying herself as she wandered around the room, fingering the computer, the fax machine, his books. Finally she lowered herself into his desk chair and began to swivel it back and forth, propelling the motion with her bare feet on the silk oriental carpet. "Oh simmer down. I can keep a secret. Of course it comes with a price, as do most things in life. I want the organization you work for to drive the bikers out of my territory."

Shocked, he gulped for air. "Be sensible woman! It would mean a war. Is that what you want?"

"Whatever it takes. I won't tolerate competition. Talk to whomever you have to and tell them either they help me out or I find someone to talk to about a

67

certain dirty lab. Better yet, if they can't help me clean up my problem, then I want into your organization."

Her words signed her own death warrant, and possibly his. There was no way the Miami people would put up with this type of blackmail.

Numbed, he turned to stare through the large window of his office. A young woman moved about on the patio, sweeping up the broken glass and righting the overturned table. It must be the Ukrainian whore Rosa had brought in. She was a pretty thing. He could see why Rosa had decided to bring her to Canada.

CHAPTER SEVEN

Stan hunched his shoulders and pulled his ragged baseball cup lower on his greasy hair. It had been three weeks since he'd entered the lower strata of Winnipeg society, and he was now a familiar face in the north end of the city. He was Dimitri Bolenko, a Ukrainian sailor who had jumped ship in Halifax a couple of months earlier.

As he approached the soup kitchen, the door swung open and two men stepped out.

"Hey, buddy," one hailed him with a rusty voice. "Good eats tonight." He burped loudly and joined his companion as they wove down the street.

Dimitri hated the time he spent here. What was worse, the stench of unwashed bodies or the smell of greasy vegetables wilting in the serving pans? It was a depressing place, but he knew he had to put in an appearance a couple of times a week. When you're struggling to earn a dollar, it's the logical solution to starvation.

He spent his days cruising the area around Main and Logan, and occasionally showed up at one of the temporary work agencies where men were hired by the hour, no work papers needed. In the evenings he visited bars and strip joints, anywhere suspected gang members hung out looking for a party and a place to swap war stories. He was the new guy, the unknown quantity, so he usually sat alone as he nursed his beer. He adopted the body language of a man of the streets, willing to pass some time in conversation but who played his cards close to his chest.

He entered the decrepit building, picked up a tray and joined the food service line that moved slowly towards its destination: two huge kettles of soup and several stainless steel pans of donated vegetables, mixed with thin slivers of meat. Slouching against the counter, he let his thoughts wander. He was tired today. He'd been up late the previous evening, visiting a number of hangouts. At the last pub, he'd started a conversation with a small group that he'd met several times before, and ended up sharing a few drinks. It was a big step in a very slow dance. From the hints he'd dropped, they knew he needed walking around money and wouldn't be too choosy about how he made it.

It would be good to get a lead, even a small one. This was lonely, time consuming work. He'd been in this situation before, and he knew the information he was looking for wouldn't just fall into his lap, he'd have to dig for it. And that meant taking some risks.

He hadn't had much luck when it came to information on Sinclair either. Although the man owned a couple of the places where he hung out, few people were willing to talk about him.

From somewhere in the line behind him, he heard Frank Crowser complaining to an aboriginal from a reserve up north. It was obvious from Frank's over-loud voice that he'd spent his afternoon drinking. Dimitri had come to know the man over a couple of his visits to Harbour Light, and suspected he'd known better times in the past. A grocer? A retail clerk? He still carried himself with some style despite his reversal of fortune.

Suddenly, above the general racket in the room the name "Sinclair' stood out. Although he tried to focus on the conversation, Dimitri couldn't make out much, other than the fact that Frank's problem involved an insurance payout.

He claimed his food, then lingered by a side table that held a stack of plastic glasses and several large pitchers of water. Maybe Frank was the lead he was looking for.

As he waited, he scanned the room. The people running the kitchen had tried to give the dining area a welcome feel by adding a few glossy posters on the battered walls, but these random splashes of colour did little to offset the harsh fluorescent lighting, worn-out linoleum, and general air of defeat that permeated the room.

At a nearby table a woman's voice rose in anger. The sound of a slap was followed quickly by a child's wail. Living out of homeless shelters and soup kitchens didn't make for good family relations.

Once Frank found a seat at one of the battered tables, Dimitri followed and sat across from him. After a nod of greeting, Frank hunched over the bowl of steaming bean soup, one dirty hand wrapped around a slice of dark bread and devoured his food. They ate the meal in silence then Dimitri let his spoon clatter to the table to catch Frank's attention. "Hey, Frank! How about you and I go and toss back a few?"

The bleary eyes across the table focused on Dimitri. "Yah, yah sure! You got the money, big talker?"

"I was lucky today," Dimitri replied with a smile. He rose and headed for the door with Frank in tow. "I caught a shift stacking some boxes over at DeFehr Furniture. Can't let it burn a hole in my pocket, you know." He patted his right front pocket, pushed the door open and headed down Main Street.

It felt good to get outside in the fresh air. The late afternoon sun threw soft purple shadows over the street as he set off in the direction of the Astoria Hotel. The traffic was heavy with commuters funnelling out of the downtown core to their homes in the suburbs, so they waited for the traffic light to change on Logan before crossing the street.

What would it be like to have a nine to five job? The thought held a lot of appeal. Clean clothes, clean bed to sleep in, and perhaps a warm meal waiting for him at the end of the day.

The anticipation of a few free drinks loosened Frank's tongue, and he launched into his life story before the light flashed to green.

"Yes siree. Used to own a mighty fine little business. My old lady worked as my bookkeeper, and we even had us a couple of part-time salesmen. It wasn't a fancy store, mind you, but it did pretty well for us."

"Yah? So what happened? Your old lady take off with one of the salesmen?"

"Nah. Nothing like that." Frank hunched his shoulders and jammed his hands into his pockets.

Dimitri didn't push him. The whole night lay ahead of them.

Located near the railway station, the Astoria was originally built to cater to well-heeled travelers. Today, the city paid for the hotel guests who desperately needed cheap welfare housing. The Astoria's second source of income came from liquor sales in the bar. Labourers from local construction crews, streetwalkers, bikers and occasionally patrons of the soup kitchen with a few dollars in their pockets came there for drinks. Dimitri wasn't a stranger here, but today he had a drinking partner.

They found a small table near the door, and Dimitri placed their order with a gum-chewing waitress. "We'll have a round of beer, Canadian okay with you, Frank?"

Frank nodded. "Why not make that two each, eh? Save her coming back right away."

Rock music blared in air rank with stale beer, a smell that spanned the ages since men first congregated in public drinking houses.

After the second beer, Frank opened up and related how a fire had destroyed the small hardware store he and his wife owned. The insurance company had refused to pay the claim on a technicality, and his wife couldn't take the stress. She had developed cancer and hadn't lived out the year. Dimitri slouched in his chair, nursed his beer and lent a sympathetic ear. He already knew how the story would play out. Misery came in all shapes and sizes, but one thing about it remained constant, it destroyed. It tore apart lives and turned some otherwise good men into alcoholics.

Although his attention centred on Frank, he was still aware of the action around them. Two distinct groups occupied their own space in the room. Congregated at the bar, a group of construction workers cracked dirty jokes and made lewd remarks to the bored waitresses. Around a cluster of tables at

73

the far end, a very different group gathered; they were members of a biker gang who wore their colours proudly on their leather jackets for everyone to see. The waitresses were quick to deliver drinks to their tables and were just as quick to leave. A few women mixed with the men, some appeared to be girlfriends but Dimitri thought the others were prostitutes.

On one of his previous visits to this bar he'd struck up a conversation with a couple of the bikers, and one of the women had tried to pick him up that same night. He'd given her a good-natured rebuff, and now she blew him a kiss across the room. He grinned broadly and raised his bottle in acknowledgement. Too late, he noticed the scowl on the face of one of her companions.

At Dimitri's elbow, Frank's story continued. Suddenly the name he was waiting for stood out in the monologue" James Sinclair.

". . . because of that bastard, James Sinclair, and his First Home Insurance company."

"Who? Who's this Sinclair?"

"James Sinclair? Oh, right. You're not from around here. Sinclair has his hand in anything and everything that produces money here in the city." Frank went on in his boozy voice, filling Dimitri in on the various negative qualities of James Sinclair. This time Dimitri gave him his full attention.

As they talked, the waitress returned several times and Dimitri continued to order, although he was only on his second beer. Frank took care of the rest.

". . . worst slum landlord. That dirty piece of shit should try livin' for a while in one of those hellholes he calls apartments instead of in that fancy house out there in Tuxedo. He's got his dirty fingers into warehouses, a trucking company . . . just about everything! You know, that blood sucker should be behind bars, or better yet, six feet under." He underscored the venom in his last comment with a deep belch and reached for yet another beer.

"I agree!" Dimitri slammed his hand down hard on the table. "A piece of shit like that shouldn't be walking around!" Lowering his voice, he added: "Bet there's a lot of others who feel the same way."

"You betcha! Hell, there's this old guy I know over at the lab who would even love to cut old lady Sinclair's throat! Hey, Taras is a Ukrainian too! Geez, this town is crawling with you Ukes."

Dimitri sucked in his breath. Frank was a goldmine of information! "You mean that new federal lab?"

"Yah, yah. That new lab over on Arlington St. Where they do all those fancy tests and keep the mega germs. Anyway, Taras Podricki worked at Sinclair's place as a gardener for a couple of years. Then the War Crimes Commission comes to town with that French-Canadian Judge. Right away all the Ukrainians, Croats and hell knows who else become suspects." One of Frank's stubby thumbs shredded the label on his beer until it hung in ribbons down the side of the bottle. "Tara told me one day he's rakin' leaves and old lady Sinclair comes out. Starts giving him the evil eye and asks him if he fought for or against the Germans. Wouldn't leave him alone. Taras quit his job. He claims that even a hint of suspicion like that could ruin his life, like it did for that poor old sod in

Ontario, Odynsky, or whatever his name was. So, now he's workin' at the lab as a night janitor."

Around them the rhythm of the bar played on. The majority of the construction crew left, to be replaced by three young men in their early twenties. Bursts of laughter or loud curses occasionally came from the leathered group at the end of the room. At one point, two girls became engaged in a spat and one left, swearing loudly. It was the girl who had blown him the kiss. As she passed their table, she ran her fingers across the back of Dimitri's neck and winked at him. He put a goofy grin on his face and winked back.

He continued to probe Frank, hoping he wasn't too far-gone in the suds to give him more information. "This guy, Taras, does he know a lot of the Ukes here? Maybe he can help me get a job." With a small chuckle, he continued lightly. "Maybe I'll even be able to find some long lost relative."

"Could be. Taras seems to know all the Ukes in this town. He lives on Jarvis, just north of Main Street. There's a teacup reader on the main floor and he lives upstairs. A teacup reader," Frank spluttered in laughter, sending a faint shower of spittle flying over the table. "What a joke! Well, whatever makes you look legal. Hey! Ya' got enough in them pockets for another beer?"

Frank couldn't provide much more information, and an hour later Dimitri helped him back to his room in a run-down boarding house.

As he left Frank's building, his instincts warned him something was wrong. A man lounged against a tree on the narrow grass margin along the sidewalk. Further down, on his left, a shadowy figure sat on

76

the steps of another aging apartment building. Without breaking stride, Dimitri turned right then another quick right to slip into the narrow space between the two buildings. Picking up speed, he sprinted through the gap and dodged around a truck in the dimly lit parking area behind the boarding house. His instincts hadn't let him down, feet pounded the sidewalk at the front of the building. *Well, I've managed to get under somebody's skin.*

As he made a quick left around a dumpster, he collided with the lookout waiting at the back door. A fist slammed into his stomach, driving the air from his lungs. He doubled over and rough hands yanked his t-shirt up, and then over his head, effectively immobilizing him. *Damn, they're pros!* His defensive training could do him no good now. The best he could do for himself was try to minimize the damage.

A blow caught him behind the knees and he fell to meet the gravel of the alley. He brought his knees up, curling into a ball. The crunch of more feet on the gravel. Boots connecting with his ribs . . . his kidneys. Red-hot pain shooting through his back . . . Grunting . . . Oblivion.

CHAPTER EIGHT

Pain prodded Dimitri back to consciousness. The overpowering reek of cheap booze surrounded him. He lay to the side of the alley against the dumpster, an empty bottle of cheap rum pressed into his hand. A good portion of the liquor coated his face and hair and soaked the front of his shirt. To anyone passing by he looked, and smelled, like a drunk deep into his bottle.

Before he dared move, he cautiously assessed the damage. His head, face and arms were fine. All of the blows had been directed at his body and legs, where his clothing would cover the bruises. Someone wanted to deliver a personal message; they weren't making a public statement. Nothing appeared to be broken, so it was a warning.

Suppressing a groan, he eased himself to his feet. A wave of nausea gripped him, and he leaned against the stinking dumpster until it passed. After several attempts, his battered legs agreed to carry him to his apartment. There would be time enough later to figure out who wanted to send a message, and why.

For the next few days he lay low, going out for an occasional meal at the greasy spoon restaurant around the corner where he also used the phone to make a report to his cover team. His bruises made their slow transition from black-and-blue to a nasty yellow. He'd soon be back in shape to continue the investigation. But who had sent the heavy-handed message? Two possibilities came to mind.

His probing, although cautious, was making someone nervous. But none of the bikers he'd made contact with seemed overly suspicious. Wary, yes, but he was a stranger so he expected a little wariness. He felt he was making steady progress with the group, to the point that he was hailed by name when he entered a few of the bars on the strip.

Another possibility came to mind, the girl at the bar who had tried to pick him up, and later blew him the kiss. She might not be a prostitute. She could be a girl with a jealous boyfriend, but on the make for a new guy. His attackers had taken pains to make sure he didn't see their faces. They could be members of the group in the bar willing to carry a message for a buddy.

Beating or not, he wasn't giving up on the investigation, but before pushing any harder in that area, he decided to make contact with the Ukrainian community. Several bars frequented by Ukrainians were located further up Main Street, and now there was possibility of contact through the old man, Taras Podricki. He made a mental note to ignore women blowing kisses, just to be on the safe side.

When he could move without pain again, he contacted the cover team to tell them he was back in business. Rudy Savage, one of the team's older members, answered the phone.

"I'm glad you called. We have something you might want to follow-up on."

"Give it to me. I'm ready to get back on the streets. I've had enough of sitting around staring at the walls."

Rudy chuckled, then replied: "We've been watching the Sinclair house and have noticed a pattern. Every Thursday a coupla' guys arrive and the hired help goes out. Once it was for a walk. Another time she went down to the strip mall for a coffee. Looks like she's been told to take a powder for a few hours."

"That is interesting. Thanks, Rudy. Tomorrow's Thursday. I think I'll go hang around the neighbourhood and try for a chance meeting. What can you tell me about her?"

"In her twenties. Pretty, in a dark sort of way. Dark hair. She looks a bit lost and doesn't talk to anyone."

The next day, Dimitri decided he'd better smarten up his image if he was going to try and strike up a conversation with a female. After a shower and a change of clothes, he used a nail file on the dirt under his nails then examined himself in the small clouded mirror of his rented room. This was the man he preferred to be. Perhaps he should set a date when he would get out of undercover work and take on something new. Maybe not a desk job, but something other than getting down in the dirt with the dogs of society. His mother had an expression that fit his current situation: "Si vous couchez avec les chiens, vous levez avec les puces." If you lie down with dogs, you get up with fleas. The thought brought a nostalgic smile to his face.

He ran a comb through the wet tangle of his hair. Weeks of relative inactivity and time spent in bars had made subtle changes to the dockworker from Vancouver. His thick brown hair was now longer, and with the constant use of a baseball cap the sun bleaching had faded. Because he skipped a lot of meals he was still slim, but the muscles in his shoulders had softened; he would no longer be seen as a man used to hard physical labour.

Late in the afternoon he was back on the street, where he wandered and window-shopped his way to Portage Avenue, then caught a bus to the Tuxedo area of the city.

As he rode, Taras Podricki came to mind. Since the evening he'd spent with Frank at the Astoria, he'd made several trips to case the aging apartment building where the teacup reader lived on the main floor. He was reasonably certain he had identified Taras Podricki. The man worked the night shift and slept well into the afternoon. He usually did a bit of grocery shopping each day and, on one occasion, he spent a full afternoon and early evening in the teacup reader's apartment.

Dimitri planned that if nothing came of his overtures to any of the gang members over the next few days, he'd start to pursue the connection to the lab through Taras Podricki.

He got off the bus on Wellington Crescent and worked his way toward the Sinclair home on a tree-lined side street. The area was peaceful: graceful houses with curving driveways set back on large lots. Within minutes of his settling on a bus stop bench with a clear view of the Sinclair driveway, several cars arrived at the house. A few minutes later, a young woman left and set off down the street. Rudy's information was accurate.

Now there's a good-looker. But it was more than her looks that caught his attention. She had a vitality about her, an energy that spoke of intelligence. She walked with a sense of purpose toward Kenaston Boulevard. Dimitri left a prudent distance between them and kept to the opposite side of the street.

At the strip mall her determination seemed to fade away. She entered a bakery that boasted a coffee bar, looked at the pastries and left. The upscale restaurant at the end of the mall seemed to tempt her, but she strolled past the door several times, then turned away. Finally, she entered. He watched through the window as the hostess lead her to a booth, before tugging the door open.

"For one, sir?" the hostess asked. "Yes, please. Would you mind if I took that table there?" Dimitri pointed to a table near the booth where the young woman sat.

The hostess glanced at the girl, then back at Dimitri with a knowing smile, "Of course!"

His salivary glands sprang into action at the sight of a roast beef dinner set before a diner at another table. If the girl ordered more than a coffee and pie, he would have time for a full meal as well. He could almost taste baked potato, awash in melted butter and sour cream.

A waitress approached the girl's booth with the menu. She shook her head. "Coffee and pie, please," she said in heavily accented English.

"I'm sorry," the waitress said as she took the menu back. "We have a minimum charge after five o'clock." It was obvious the young woman didn't understand what was happening and again asked for coffee, this time miming taking a drink and adding another phrase. A look of frustration crossed her face.

It was then that Dimitri realized she was speaking Ukrainian. "Perhaps I can help," he said as he rose from his seat and approached her booth. "I believe the young lady is Ukrainian." Turning to the seated girl he explained the problem in her language.

Embarrassment flooded her face as she quickly rose to her feet. For a moment she appeared very young and vulnerable, totally overwhelmed by the situation. Acting on impulse, Dimitri steered her to his table and gently pushed her into the empty chair. "I'm eating alone and I'd welcome some company. Please, join me for a cup of coffee," he said in Ukrainian. Before she could protest he turned to the waitress and ordered the dinner special, two coffees and two pieces of pie.

"You're very kind, but I don't want to intrude on your meal." Embarrassment reddened her face. "I didn't realize I couldn't order just a coffee and pie in here. I feel so foolish." When the flush subsided the look that followed was one of misery. She was on the verge of tears. The coffee arrived, and she didn't protest when he urged her to relax and enjoy the hot drink.

"You're new to Winnipeg, and Canada as well?"

She nodded and wrapped her arms around herself as if warding off an internal chill.

"Cheer up, I'm a newcomer here too. Believe me, the newness will wear off." He leaned forward, his elbows on the table, as he observed his new companion. "My name is Dimitri, by the way. And what shall I call you? Miss Pie and Coffee, perhaps?" His small joke and light manner brought a smile to her face, and she let her eyes meet his for the first time.

"Sonja. Sonja Sepsik. You're very kind, and I appreciate your help. I was out for a walk and thought I'd treat myself. I feel very stupid really. I should perhaps stick to ordering things I can just point to. Like an ice cream cone. This place seemed so attractive, I . . ."

The lights in the restaurant highlighted the copper strands in her hair and pooled in the hollows under her cheekbones. She was more than pretty, she was beautiful, and it felt good to be in her company. Dimitri would do whatever he could to stall her, just for the pleasure of her company.

"You're not intruding on my meal. It's nice to hear Ukrainian again. Now, how is it, Sonja, that you are here in Winnipeg and you don't speak English?" He smiled in an effort to encourage her.

Her gaze dropped to her lap. The hand with the cup that had barely made the journey to her mouth returned to the table. "Have you been in Canada long?" she countered with her own question.

No wedding ring. Good quality clothes. Yet obviously reluctant to talk about herself. He'd try another tactic. "Not long." He made a show of looking around the restaurant, as though to be certain no one was eavesdropping, then he dropped his voice to a conspiratorial whisper and leaned in closer to her. "Actually, I jumped ship in Halifax and I've been working my way west. I kind of like Winnipeg though. Lots of Ukrainians here and a fellow can get lost in the crowd, so to speak. What about you?"

His supper arrived and his stomach growled in anticipation. Her laugh brought a sparkle to her eyes and relaxed the tense muscles of her face and shoulders.

"You're in the country illegally? You're joking, no?" He shook his head and this time she believed him. Perhaps finding some reassurance in that fact, she began to talk. "I've been here for a month. I'm from Ushgorod, in Ukraine. Do you know where that is?"

He shook his head but didn't speak.

"There's no opportunity there for young people. My younger brother made his way to Hungary and brought me over later but . . . he seems to have gotten mixed up with . . ." Her voice trailed off and she avoided his eyes. The waitress paused as she passed their table and refilled their cups. Sonja sipped the steaming brew, perhaps to collect her thoughts and measure the risk in telling this stranger her story.

"People can sometimes be forced by circumstances to make unwise decisions, Sonja. Your brother wouldn't be the first to make bad choices."

"This wasn't just a bad choice, Dimitri. My brother sold his soul to the devil! And worse, when I got there, I found that the people he worked for had paid my way to Hungary. I owed them, and . . ." The muscles of her throat convulsed to keep the sobs from escaping and once again tears welled in her eyes and threatened to overflow.

The enormity of her situation hit Dimitri full force. She had been sold. Betrayed by her own brother. He resisted the impulse to move his hand to cover hers. She might take the gesture the wrong way.

He had finished his meal. An alert waitress removed the dish and replaced it with the two plates of pie.

The interruption helped Sonja regain her composure. She shrugged. "No matter. I'm here now and I'll soon learn to speak English. Then I'll be okay."

In an attempt to lighten her mood, Dimitri laughed softly. "You said "okay.' That's a very English word. I see your lessons have already started."

Sonja smiled, and then shyly ducked her head. A lot had gone unsaid in their conversation, but he wasn't about to push her. Nevertheless, he was intrigued by her and her situation. How had she ended up in Winnipeg? What was she doing here? "So, that's why you've come to the restaurant, to practice your English?"

"No, not really. Well . . . I was told to get out a bit. To go for a cup of coffee, that it might help me with my English. But I know that wasn't the real reason. I think the people I'm staying with wanted me out of the house. Rosa's husband was having a special meeting with some business people. He seems very fussy about those meetings."

Dimitri gripped his dessert fork tightly in his hand. If he could keep her talking, she could be a gold mine of information. "Rosa?" He feigned only mild curiosity. "She's a relative?"

A look of pain crossed her face and she shook her head. "No. Mrs. Sinclair is the one who arranged for me to come to Canada." She finished the coffee but hadn't touched the pie. She checked her watch.

His briefing papers had mentioned that Sinclair's wife ran massage parlours and was involved in prostitution. It all fit. But this girl didn't look, or act, like a prostitute. Maybe he was getting ahead of himself here. He needed more information.

It was obvious Sonja wanted to leave, yet was too polite to rush him. If he took his time over his coffee, then offered to walk her back, perhaps he'd have a few extra minutes with her.

The pie was cherry, not one of his favourites, but he feigned great pleasure in it as he ate slowly. They chatted about things to see and do in Winnipeg. Finally, her nervousness got the better of her.

"I'm sorry, but I should be getting back. They may be worried if I'm out too late."

"Of course. I was enjoying your company so much, I didn't realize I was keeping you. May I walk you back to the house? It's nice to talk to someone in Ukrainian."

Her initial smile turned to a look of caution. "Perhaps just half way."

He paid the bill, then they made their way out of the restaurant into the humid night.

Seeming more comfortable in his presence than at first, she filled him in on some of the details of her escape from the Ukraine and her time in Budapest, but she made no further mention of Rosa Sinclair.

"My brother says I may have a relative in Canada. Somewhere in Manitoba. Is Manitoba a large province?"

"A large province, but with only a few people if you compare it to a country in Europe. Winnipeg has a large Ukrainian population though."

They chatted for several blocks, then she turned to him. "It might be better if I went on my own from here. But I would like to thank you for the pie and coffee."

He didn't want to say goodbye, and not only because she had a lot of information about the Sinclairs to share. "Tell you what, Sonja. How about we meet again, for coffee. I just might know someone who can help you find your missing relative. Do you think it would be okay if I gave you a call? I mean, would the Sinclairs mind if you received phone calls there?"

She turned her face to him smiling with obvious pleasure. He felt the warmth of it deep in his gut.

"I'd enjoy that. If you call during the day I'm usually the only one home. Rosa would be delighted if my English improved."

The last was said with a slight laugh. Although tinged with regret, it was still a laugh, and it fell pleasantly on Dimitri's ear. "Good. Then you'll give me your phone number?"

She seemed startled for a moment, then flustered. "Oh . . . of course. But I have no pen. I put my money in my pocket when I left the house."

"No problem. I can find it in the phone book. What name should I look under?" He felt a tinge of guilt at how easily the question slid across his tongue.

"James Sinclair," she replied. She raised her hand in farewell as she turned and walked down the street.

Dimitri smiled. He now had the perfect excuse to meet with Sonja again, and to pay a call on Taras Podricki.

CHAPTER NINE

The warmth of the summer day faded as a cooling breeze and huge thunderclouds bullied their way in from the west. James Sinclair eyed the horizon trying to gauge how much time remained before the storm hit. Probably about an hour. Time enough for Ralf Altmann and him to finish their golf game and make it to the clubhouse for a beer before the downpour.

They were approaching the eleventh hole of the Pine Ridge Golf Course, yet he still hadn't found the courage to bring up the subject of Rosa. He knew he couldn't ignore her threat and hope she would back down; Rosa didn't make idle threats. And if he was going to pass her ultimatum along to anyone in the organization, Altmann, his immediate superior, was the obvious choice.

Altmann, born Randolfo Altano in Italy, had arrived in Canada in the late sixties. With help from his family's unlimited resources and his own keen mind, he now controlled an empire that made James' success look puny in comparison. James was normally a confident man who took pride in his accomplishments and it galled him to no end that he felt insignificant in Altmann's company. Altmann controlled corporations that gave generous funding to sports events, charitable organizations and political parties. In an effort to measure up, James made his own charitable donations, but he knew they were small change in Altmann's eyes.

Altmann's voice broke into his thoughts. "So, James, I suspect you have a problem that you want to discuss with me. You certainly didn't get me out here to improve your golf game. Out with it, man."

There it was. Like it or not, he had to get the whole sorry-ass mess out into the open. Drawing a deep breath, James cleared his throat several times before he answered. "There seems to be some increasing tension between rival factions in the prostitution business."

"And one of those "rival factions,' as you so succinctly put it, is your own Rosa." Altmann slid the comment in so smoothly he could have been discussing the condition of the fairway.

Adrenalin shot through James' veins. Had Rosa already been dropping hints around town that she had the force of the organization behind her? It was possible . . . but not probable. The smartest course of action for her was to let the bikers think the heat was coming from some other corner of the playing field. Then if there was retaliation it wouldn't be aimed at her. Rosa was more than smart; she was cunning.

He'd met her while working as a croupier in a Las Vegas casino. She'd run a minor call-girl ring and done a little dancing on the side in a few of the splashy Vegas productions. The pair hit it off. She was beautiful and had brains. She'd figured out a way for James to fix the odds in her favour when she played his table, and they shared the winnings. They were young and daring, and for a while they lived high, at least until security picked up on the scam. They fled to Canada with a tidy bundle to help set them up.

91

Rosa felt comfortable in her line of work but encouraged James to branch out into legitimate businesses. Over the years they'd both done well, but now Rosa was getting greedy and careless. Or maybe she felt threatened by James' success.

When he could trust his voice again, he spoke. "Well . . . you know I operate quite independently from Rosa. I have no control over""

"James, James, James. Please, don't give me that," Altmann broke in smoothly as he teed up his next shot. "Of course you have control over her. She's your wife. And unfortunately your wife has been snooping around in places where she shouldn't. I got a call from Miami. They've followed a line of enquiry back to your Rosa. That kind of attention isn't good for the Winnipeg division, now, is it?" He swung, and his shot flew clean and straight, right down the middle of the fairway. A three iron would land him on the green.

They already know! They've probably been waiting to see how long it took me to bring it to their attention. James wiped his sweat-slick hands and grabbed at the first wood he spotted in his bag. "She's only picked up bits and pieces, Ralf. She doesn't really know what's going on, and I sure as hell haven't told her anything. I admit, she's been snooping, and now she's pressuring me to use the organization to put heat on the bikers. They're crowding her area downtown and she wants them out."

He moved to the tee box to set up his shot, already knowing it would be a disaster. How do you put a nail in your wife's coffin and play a decent round of golf at the same time? His swing was tight and the ball ploughed into the bush near the 125-yard marker.

"And if the bikers aren't muscled out she'll leak a few secrets?" They made their way back to the cart and Altmann steered it down the gravelled path to the area where James' ball had disappeared into a stand of oaks.

James debated forfeiting a stroke then decided that might be taken as an indication of his character. Better to search out the damn thing and see if he could play it. It wasn't overly hot, but a band of perspiration dampened his forehead. The day was a nightmare, the game an agony. Gritting his teeth, he searched the rough and came up empty. He played another ball, and again wasn't satisfied with the effort.

"Just isn't your day, is it, James? Rosa's a threat, and we'll have to deal with it before Miami takes matters into their own hands. You know the rules, and the rules won't be broken because the threat comes from your family."

James' chest constricted, and he forced himself to take a deep breath. The implication was clear. Although he was expecting it, the decision was still difficult to accept. His love for Rosa had died years ago, but there was still a lot of shared history there. It hadn't been all bad. In fact, without her pushing him, he wouldn't be what he was today. What am I today? No ...don't go down that road.

Nothing was said of a sanction against him; then again his business ventures in Winnipeg were a key link in the organization's chain. Still, they were letting him off easy.

Ralf stopped the cart on the path near his ball. With an easy swing of a three iron, he put the ball on the green.

James decided to make a plea, despite realizing he was working with a very weak hand. "Ralf, I don't think this has to be dealt with""

"Stop right there. The organization can't live with this threat hanging over its head. You're part of the problem, James." Altmann eased the cart to a stop on the path parallel to Sinclair's ball and turned to face him. His hooded eyes held no emotion as he spoke. "So you will have a direct hand in the solution. You see, we need to know where your loyalties lie with respect to the organization."

Thunder roared directly overhead, and the world around him went misty. From a distance, he heard Altmann call his name, and then his vision cleared. No, not thunder. The roaring was in his head. He gripped the dash for support as Altmann signalled the group behind them to play through.

***

The following day, James placed a call to Laurence O'Connor. He cringed at the thought of Laury's reaction when his cell phone rang. There were only a few people who knew the number, and Laury wouldn't be expecting an unscheduled call.

"Laury, I wonder if you would be free for lunch this afternoon, say twelve-fifteen? I'll reserve a table at Dubrovnik's, if you can make it." He could hear that his voice sounded strained, and he made a conscious effort to keep it firm.

"This is pretty short notice, James. Can we make it twelve-thirty? That would be better for me. I'll see you then."

James replaced the receiver with unsteady hands. Could there be repercussions from a public meeting? Miami wanted as little contact as possible between the members. Each unit worked independently and the strands were woven together at the top, in Miami. For all intents and purposes Laury and James moved in different social circles. They did meet occasionally at various functions, most recently at a reception when James donated two hundred thousand dollars to the University of Manitoba Library fund. Their business contact, however, remained behind closed doors. James shrugged mentally. Two businessmen having lunch at one of the best restaurants in town shouldn't attract undue attention.

Now that he could think clearly again, he reviewed yesterday's events on the golf course. For a while there, he'd thought he was having a heart attack. He'd tried to reason with Altmann, but the decision remained unchanged. They actually expected him to get rid of his own wife!

"The organization has its own enforcers!" He had pleaded.

"Yes, we do. But if you do the job, we know you'll keep your mouth shut when the questions start getting tough."

"I'll be one of the first suspects! What if I get arrested? Ralf, you know that my transportation companies are the key to the success of our very lucrative business dealings. Without me, that link at the airport is down the tubes and there's no way to get those fragile shipments out of Winnipeg. Sure, Laury might have access to organs, but without someone on the inside to move that cargo, the sale dies before it gets off the ground."

"We'll put one of our best lawyers on it if it comes to that. Relax, James. If you handle things properly, suspicion won't even fall on you. Remember, we've got Laury in the lab. Find someone who's expendable to take the fall, someone no one will miss. Laury can work the rest out for you." Then Ralf smiled and slapped James on the back.

James had tossed and turned all night, his brain ploughing through different scenarios: a convenient car accident, no good. He'd have to hire someone to tinker with the car. A drive-by shooting, again, he'd have to involve someone else. Today he still wrestled with the problem, and lack of sleep didn't help. Furthermore, Altmann's advice to "relax' grated.

He paced the small area of his home office. When he met with Laury at noon he needed to have some kind of plan in place. Ideally the fall guy would be someone who knew Rosa and had reason to hate her. Of course, it could be set up to appear she caught someone in the act of burglarizing the house. No, too complicated.

He needed someone expendable. A movement at the pool caught his eye. It was Sonja, Rosa's new recruit, straightening out the poolside furniture. Now there's someone expendable! She's new in Winnipeg, doesn't know anyone, and can't speak the language. It would be easy to set it up to have her take the fall. But motive? To hear Rosa tell it, the girl should be grateful that Rosa pulled her out of a nasty situation, that wouldn't work.

As he continued pacing, his desperation grew. Maybe I could report that the girl wanted to go back, and Rosa refused to let her go. Better yet, Rosa caught her stealing. No, that won't work. That would have to involve a witness. Come on, come on! Think! This has to come together and it has to come together fast!

What about the pool boy? Now there's a sneaky looking little bastard.

He moved to the window and watched as Sonja paused by a planter to remove some weeds. Ever since Rosa and that gardener went after each other, the yard hadn't been the same. The gardener! Of course! What's his name? Taras Podricki! The motive is already set up. He hates Rosa and has a questionable background. Something to do with the Nazis. When he left he'd asked Rosa for a reference, said he was applying for a janitorial position at the new lab. When Rosa refused the reference, James had given him one.

Would it work? He tossed a few scenarios around and could find no fault with them. But which was better . . . the girl or the old man. In the end he settled on the old man. The girl was young and pretty. A jury might feel more sympathy for her if she turned on the tears. Who would care about an old man, a suspected Nazi?

By the time James arrived at Dubrovnik's for lunch, he had the semblance of a plan.

The waiter seated them at a table in a quiet corner of the dining room. The beautiful restaurant sat along the west bank of the river in an older part of town. Normally, a lunch at Dubrovnik's was a time to unwind and enjoy one of the best meals to be found in Winnipeg. Around them the muted sounds of table conversations were overlaid with the sounds of cutlery on fine china, and soft classical music. Today James took no pleasure in his surroundings.

"Red or white wine, Laury?"

"Neither for me. You go ahead though."

They made several attempts at idle conversation during the meal, but James found it difficult to concentrate on inconsequential chatter. Twice, he was about to bring up the subject that dominated his thoughts, then lost his nerve. Why the hell didn't Laury probe a little . . . give him an opening? It wasn't until the waiter set a steaming cappuccino in front of Laury that James found the nerve to come to the point of the meeting.

"I'm in trouble and I need your help," he stated bluntly as he twisted the stem of his wine glass between his fingers. "As far as the organization goes, we're both insignificant little foot soldiers and we're expected to follow orders. I've . . . well, I've been given an order that requires some assistance from you."

Warily, Laury nodded for James to continue.

He took a guarded look around the restaurant to ensure they were out of earshot from any of the other diners, then lowered his voice. "My wife, Rosa, has become a threat to our business dealings. I've been told to take care of the problem."

Laury's cup clattered back into the saucer, and his breath exploded from his pursed lips. Leaning across the table, he lowered his voice to barely above a whisper.

"What? That's insane! You'd be the first person the police suspect."

"And that's where you come in," James' voice carried more conviction than he actually felt. Perhaps if he played the part, the confidence would follow. "You're going to have to help me frame another suspect."

Laury seemed to have recovered from his initial shock. He settled back into his chair and quickly scanned the room. No one was paying any particular attention to their table. "I still don't like it, but I take it you have someone in mind?"

James nodded and took a large swallow of wine. He found it difficult to articulate something that, up to now, had only been a plan in his mind. Once spoken, it would become fact, and once fact, it would be set in motion.

The enormity of his situation hit him again with full force. He was a puppet in a stage show in which someone else pulled the strings. It was no use trying to sever the strings. He had given over control of them when he became a member of the organization. The show would go on, even if he were no longer a willing member of the production.

"Yes, my former gardener. He's been working at the lab for the last couple of months as a night janitor. His name is Taras Podricki." His throat was suddenly dry, but he realized with some surprise that his wine glass was empty. He sipped from his water glass.

"Oh, sure. Old Podricki. I didn't realize he used to work for you."

"When the War Crimes Commission came to Winnipeg, Rosa practically accused him of being a

99

Nazi. Even asked him if he had a swastika tattoo under his arm. He blew up and they had a confrontation. That's when he went to work at the lab." James remembered Rosa's glee as she described the argument

"My plan hinges on his coming back to trim the hedges when I call him. I'm going to tell him I'm desperate, that they haven't been trimmed properly since he left. The old codger seems to have a real love for gardening, and his argument was with Rosa, not me, so I'm banking on him coming to do the work."

James took a deep breath and toyed with his coffee spoon. The heavy feeling from yesterday crept back into his chest. He continued with difficulty. "His footprints will be around the windows and the little patio that leads off the garden-doors of our bedroom. Later, I'll break the glass . . ." He realized he didn't need to tell Laury the full plan. It was too difficult to articulate it anyway.

Laury seemed uneasy, and for a wild moment James thought he might refuse to help. Finally, he nodded.

When he spoke, his voice carried heavy resignation. "I'll say this again . . . I don't like it. But, as you said, we're in this together. What do you need from me?"

"Just get me a few strands of Podricki's hair. You must have access to his locker at the lab. Then, when the hairs come through the lab for that precious DNA analysis everyone puts so much stock in, keep your eye on them. If we control the process, it has to come out in our favour."

100

They sat in the restaurant for another half-hour, fine tuning the details, then paid their bill and went their separate ways. James opted for a walk along the riverbank walkway behind Dubrovnik's before heading back to his office. He could clear his head but it would be harder to clear his conscience.

CHAPTER TEN

As Laury eased the Lexus out of the restaurant's parking lot, he turned the situation over in his mind. It would be naive to believe that Sinclair's request came from anywhere but the top. While saying "no' was not an option, with careful planning he could eliminate the risks to himself and maybe even use the situation to his advantage.

Once again his thoughts turned to Anel. She was still an unknown factor, and the unknown didn't sit well with him. He liked things laid out clearly and neatly. Packaged. No loose ends. Maybe he'd read her wrong and she was holding out for marriage.

Maybe marriage wasn't such a bad idea after all. She would be legally attached to him, could never testify against him, if it came to that. He'd watched her on both a personal and professional level, and she handled the specimens with expert ease. More importantly, she didn't have a suspicious nature and took his experiments in transplant immunology at face value. Although his plans wouldn't come to a dead end without her, it would be a lot easier to assign her to certain cases, and certain samples, if he knew he had her on his side.

Dead ends. The thought brought his stepfather to mind.

"Don't be so stupid, Laurence. If you have to choose chemistry, why not specialize in a lucrative field, like fossil fuel research? There's some good money to be made there. But medical biochemistry? It's a dead end road, for God's sake!"

"You've got to be kidding!" Laury replied, not even trying to keep the incredulity out of his voice. "Fossil fuel research is as dead as the fossils being studied. I want to be part of a science that's going to improve the quality of man's life. Every month you hear an announcement of some big breakthrough in biochemistry. As a field of research, medical biochemistry is set to explode and I'm going to be part of it!" The realist and the young idealist seldom found common ground.

Laury was a natural for the study of chemistry, and took great pride in graduating with honours. Grampton University was quick to offer him a position to serve as research assistant to Professor Ivan Sastushyn. He thought he'd caught the brass ring. What an idiot he'd been back then. The idealist in him was sure he'd discover the magic drug that would lessen the world's suffering. For three stinking years he worked with Ivan on that new base compound, and for what? It was his work that finally made the breakthrough, but it was Ivan Sastushyn who took the credit and won the accolades. There was no mention of Laurence O'Connor.

Three years of promises, three years of dreams, three years of his life gone forever. And for what? He could still remember the bitterness he'd felt that day. But the death of his idealism created a void, and that void was soon filled by ambition. DNA research was now the "darling' field to be in, and he gravitated toward it. Grants were readily available and the payoff for sharp researchers who could work the system was good. Better yet, he was able to make contacts with people who admired his ambition and were willing to pass his name up the pipeline. When the organization from Miami contacted him, they provided much more than a financial incentive; they provided the recognition any disenchanted idealist was more than willing to embrace.

Laury was so deep in thought that his car nearly collided with an SUV exiting the lab's parking lot. Muttering under his breath, but with a forced smile on his face, he waved the startled driver through the gate and edged the Lexus into his parking stall. "Director' the nameplate read. Director, he thought with secret delight. I'm director of a hell of a lot more than most people give me credit for!

As he headed for the building, he passed Anel's Grand Am in its stall. He paused for a moment, then made a decision. He'd get more aggressive with her. If she didn't come around in another couple of weeks, he'd have to write her off as a waste of time. There were other, more pliable girls in the lab who would be eager to spend time with their director in exchange for a little discretion. Pamela immediately came to mind.

The elevator rose smoothly to the second floor and the doors eased open. It was time to put in motion the plan to implicate the old janitor, Taras Podricki. James would owe him, big time, for this.

He found Anel in her small glassed cubicle finishing off paperwork. She raised her head to greet him and although a smile rose to her lips, it did not light up her eyes. It was a friendly smile, nothing more.

104

He waved a greeting. "Anything happen while I was out?"

"Some samples came in from the crime scene on Spence Street. A couple of them were wipes, and I've stabilized them. Pamela's doing the chemical analysis with the ICR-MS."

"The ICR-MS." He crossed his arms and perched on the edge of her desk. "I can't remember the last time I heard anyone use the proper name for that machine. I bet you can't even remember what the initials stand for."

She laughed and dipped her head so the wings of her hair hid her face. Sunlight coming through the window highlighted the occasional lighter strand. One day he'd be able to draw his fingers through that curly mass. He was sure of it. As she straightened her head the movement stirred the air and he caught the faint odour of her perfume. It was intoxicating.

"I may not use the full name, but I work with it often enough. It stands for Ion Cyclotron Resonance Mass Spectrometer or ICR-MS for short. I trust I passed the exam?"

"You did! And you just won yourself a dinner out tonight. No," he raised his hand to stop her objection. "No arguing. A bet's a bet, and you won. What time shall I pick you up?"

Caught off guard, she acquiesced, "Seven o'clock. I can be ready by seven."

"Fine. Seven it is."

Rising, he clapped his hands together to dismiss the topic. "Now, down to business, Miss Blondeau." His tone was business-like, but the mock leer and cocked eyebrow brought a smile to her face. Then he sobered. "One of the European medical journals has a warning about those infamous beta-lactamase enzymes. Seems researchers have discovered some transference to previously non-resistant strains of bacteria. Some of the same ones that I deal with in transplant rejection, in fact."

He noted the look of worry on her face. It was going well. He paused for a moment, as though mulling over an idea, then continued. "It might be a good idea to do a study right here in the lab. Round up some samples from protected areas, maybe hallways, lockers, air-locks, that kind of thing."

She seemed to grasp his meaning immediately. "There's a lot of traffic between here and N-block. Maybe samples from random areas from the first floor up?"

Yes! His hook had worked. He had a legitimate reason to get into Podricki's locker.

Anel picked up the phone and dialled. "Security? Please send someone up to the director's office with a key card to all areas, including lockers. Director O'Connor wants to make a sweep for antibiotic resistant strains of bacteria. Yes . . . we realize personal areas require notification. We'll post notices on any lockers we open. Thanks."

Sample bags and specimen containers in hand, Anel and Laury were joined by the security officer as they made their way through the two sections, randomly selecting desks, lockers, cabinets and storage rooms. They fished out dust and swept it into small plastic bags, and did wipes with sterile gauze on air-lock handles and doorknobs as they went.

Laury made sure he examined Taras Podricki's locker personally. As he scanned the meagre contents of the narrow cubicle his tense stomach fluttered. If he did this right, the big boys in Florida would really sit up and take notice. If he screwed it up . . . well, he might as well bite down on the barrel of a revolver and pull the trigger. There was no way he would rot in jail for 20 years!

Moving quickly, he tucked a few hairs from Taras' comb into a sample bag. A white scrub coat of the kind all cleaning personnel wore, hung from one of the hooks in the locker. Laury shook it over a small square of plastic wrap, folded the wrap and tucked it into his blazer pocket. He pulled several fibres from the frayed sleeve of a tattered sweater on the second hook, added them to the hair in the bag, and slipped it into his pocket. As he hung the sweater back on the hook, he heard Anel approach from the second bank of lockers.

"The janitor moves around the building the most. I thought I'd be extra thorough here." He closed the locker and Anel taped a note to the door advising the owner that a random sweep for bacteria had been done in his locker. It wasn't an unusual note. Sweeps were done occasionally.

The small group left the locker room and moved on to the mailroom.

"Oh," Laury said as he snapped his fingers. "I forgot my pen back there. You go on, I'll catch up." Quickly, he retraced his steps and removed the notice from the locker. It wouldn't do to have the old man remember that someone had recently been in his locker.

***

The Beaujolais Restaurant in St. Boniface had an excellent reputation, and Anel felt a thrill of pleasure as Laury handed the car keys to the parking attendant. Although she passed the building occasionally, she had never dined here. The atmosphere was perfect for romance and Laury was an attentive suitor.

Always courteous, he now went out of his way to please her. He consulted the waiter for the best dish on the menu and asked the wine steward to bring a suitable wine for the meal. When a pretty girl came around selling red roses from a basket, he bought her a half-dozen tied with a velvet ribbon.

At first, she found Laury entertaining. As the evening wore on and the wine flowed, however, an unknown Laury O'Connor began to emerge. By the time the dessert arrived Anel began to feel a little uneasy.

"Did you hear the joke about the Ukrainian farmer trying to bury his dead horse?"

"No," she replied. She hadn't enjoyed his last joke and hoped this would be the end of them.

"When his neighbour asked him why he was digging so many holes, he answered, "None of them is large enough."" Laury laughed uproariously but she found it hard to force a faint smile. She wanted to be a good sport, but ethnic jokes made her uncomfortable. Making fun at the expense of those who were disadvantaged was no proof of wit.

Laury seemed to realize that his joke had fallen flat and took a more intellectual approach. They began to discuss art and seemed to find a common ground in Picasso.

"I saw a reproduction of Picasso's "Woman With a Guitar' today in a gallery advertisement." He paused for another sip of his wine. "It's certainly eye-catching, but as art, it's nonsense. I guess I share your dislike for those distorted, so-called masterpieces that art critics praise."

"I said I didn't understand it, not that I disliked it," she corrected.

"That's understandable," he said as he tried to refill her wine glass. "Picasso himself said that his abstract paintings were worthless before he put his signature on them." He laughed too loudly at his own humour.

Anel refused more wine and Laury filled his glass yet again. She knew he wasn't a drinker, yet he'd ordered a cocktail before the meal and they were now into a second bottle of wine. To her embarrassment, he began to appear intoxicated. His speech was sluggish and he had taken to leaning forward with his elbows planted firmly on the table, as if for support.

"The woman who decorates my home will have a free hand as far as art and furnishings go. Would you enjoy decorating your own home Anel, or would you prefer an interior decorator?"

"I'd prefer to do it myself, I think. It would be like putting my own signature on my surroundings. It may sound silly but""

"Not at all! Your wish would be my command . . . if you were my wife. It may interest you to know that I've had plans for my dream home drawn up for some time. Would you care to see them?"

Oh dear God! Is this some form of proposal? The room closed in on her and she fought down the

109

urge to flee from the restaurant. For a fleeting instant the chair pressing against her back felt like rough wood. With hands that would barely respond to her command, she pushed her dessert aside and concentrated her attention on getting the coffee cup from the table to her lips. Ignore the comment? Make a joke of it? She couldn't, and wouldn't, acknowledge it as a serious statement and thereby give it life.

"The evening has been lovely, Laury, but I think it's time we called it a night. Look, there's our waiter. Why don't you ask him for our bill?"

With shaking fingers she dug a quarter from her purse while he settled the bill. "If you don't mind, I think it would be better if I took a cab. There's no sense you taking me all the way home and then having to drive . . ."

"What d'you mean, 'a cab!' Do you think because I've enjoyed a few drinks I'm unfit to drive?" He sounded far too determined, and Anel sensed that any further insistence on a cab would lead to a quarrel. The last thing she wanted was to create a scene.

They got no further than the Provencher Bridge before he misjudged the distance between his Lexus and the car in front of them. The impact was slight, no more than a tap, and Laury sobered up instantly.

"Anel, this is minor, I'm sure. But I do have liquor on my breath. Would you mind giving them my driver's license number and registration? It's there in the glove compartment. Tell them if there's any damage I'm more than willing to pay for it myself, rather than going through the insurance companies."

She did mind. He shouldn't have been driving, and they both knew it. Biting back a comment she might regret later, she nodded, and rummaged through the contents of the glove compartment until she found the insurance folder. He handed her his driver's license and she left the car to speak to the other driver. Thanks to solid bumpers, there appeared to be no damage to either vehicle, but she provided Laury's name and telephone number just in case they'd missed any damage in the dark.

As she opened the door to get back in the car, an envelope fluttered to the ground. She must have dislodged it from the glove compartment when she searched for the insurance papers. The courtesy light on the door clearly illuminated the envelope and the Swiss stamp on the corner. In bold letters on the return address corner she saw the words Banque Alliance de Suisse, Geneva, Switzerland.

Before she could replace the envelope in the glove compartment, Laury leaned over the width of the seat and took it from her hands. Without meeting her eyes, he shoved the envelope into his suit jacket pocket.

"I'm negotiating with a Swiss firm to buy a new electron microscope for the lab. We're using the bank to set up financing." Anel didn't believe a word of it. She knew for a fact there were no plans for a new microscope; he'd have consulted her before making such a purchase.

His speech was no longer sluggish but the accident had obviously shaken him. In an attempt to keep him off the main streets Anel made a request: "Laury, could we possibly go down Cathedral Avenue and turn off on Alnau Street? Since we're in

111

the area anyway, I'd like to drive by the house where I grew up. It's really not out of the way."

Once they were on Cathedral Avenue, there was very little traffic for Laury to contend with. As they passed through the older district, Anel drank in the peacefulness of the tree-lined streets and small homes on their narrow lots. Childhood memories overwhelmed her.

She barely realized she was speaking out loud when she commented, "Look at these little houses. Families are sitting there in their living rooms, maybe just reading, or watching television. Most of them haven't even drawn the curtains. They have no secrets""

"Stupid habit!" Laury interrupted as he turned onto Alnau Street. "People should cherish their privacy. How do they even raise a family in these toy houses?"

As they passed her family's former home, her heart constricted in sorrow for what was gone. Without conscious thought, she reached out her hand to the tiny house with its neat little patch of grass, but her hand was stopped by the glass of the luxury car's window. Within sight, but out of reach.

"Anel, come in for supper, dear."

"Coming, Momma. Can Marcel eat with us tonight?"

"If he's asked his mother. Both of you, wash those hands now. Mes petits porcs. You're as dirty as little piglets!"

"Marcel's cat has new kittens and she's hidden them under the steps. We found them!"

Marcel. It had been years since she'd thought of the boy who, when she was seven, she'd sworn to

112

love forever. He broke her heart when he started to date Susan, but who could blame him. She had shut out even Marcel when . . .

No! The past should remain in the past. It was the future she should concentrate on.

What was her future? Was it with this man beside her who had told her more than once that he cared for her? Tonight he had tested the water, she was sure of it. Perhaps she lacked the capacity to feel passionately about anyone, but should she marry because she was lonely and wanted to be needed? She didn't even know Laury. Lately he was acting differently, secretive, and tonight he appeared to be nervous about something. His gaiety seemed forced, his drinking excessive, and he'd lied about acquiring a new microscope.

Her reverie was cut short as they drew up to her unit in the modest row of townhouses where she lived. He escorted her to the door and made sure she found her key.

"I'm truly sorry that our evening was spoiled with that minor accident. You were quite right to suggest a cab, and I'm embarrassed to admit that I did drink too much with supper. Please forgive me, Anel. Perhaps you'll allow me to take you out next week to make up for this fiasco?"

He gathered her in his arms for a parting kiss but she found it far from pleasant. His mouth demanded more than she could give, and his breath was heavy with stale wine.

Once inside, she arranged the roses in a vase and placed them on the small coffee table in her living room. A family photo that she kept on the bookcase caught her eye and she picked it up. What a happy family they had been. Her mother loved her father passionately, and that love overflowed to include her. If a silver lining could be found in the darkness of their death, it was the fact that the two had died together. Neither would have wanted to live without the other.

Would her marriage be the same? It wouldn't if she married Laury, she was sure of that. Was there someone out there that she could share a love with, a love as deep as her parents' love?

The photo had been taken in the garden of the tiny house on Alnau Street. As she replaced it on the shelf she noticed the house in the background. It was the Briere home, where her friend Marcel had lived. She had thought of him twice this evening and suddenly she longed to talk with him again. He was someone from her childhood, and despite her earlier wish to shut out the past, she knew she needed to return to that time of peace and comfort that was also a time of hurt and betrayal. A time when she felt love surround her, yet she had also learned to hate. She needed to speak with someone who was "safe,' and she needed to speak about "the bad time.'

CHAPTER ELEVEN

Sonja prowled the small apartment that was originally built as a mother-in-law suite. It occupied half the basement area of the Sinclair home. The privacy arrangement worked well for her, but she was often alone and quite bored. A maid came in several times a week to clean the residence upstairs so Sonja's job consisted of tidying up between her visits. The work was hardly enough to keep her occupied, and her English was too limited to enjoy the television or the newspaper.

She was tempted to go lie in the sun at the pool, a luxury that was foreign to her, but she owned no swimsuit and she didn't know if Rosa would approve of seeing her idle. Rosa had let her know in no uncertain terms that she wasn't a guest in the house.

With so much time on her hands she found it easy to fret, to find problems where none existed. Rosa had made it clear she had plans for Sonja once her English reached conversational level, but for some reason the lessons had all but stopped. Sonja sensed something was bothering the woman, and it was clear there was a lot of tension between her and her husband. If they were having marital problems it was none of Sonja's business, but most of the arguments had something to do with Rosa's business, which could have repercussions for Sonja.

Rosa had purchased a round trip ticket for Sonja's trip to Canada. If the business was in difficulty, Rosa just might send Sonja back with the return coupon. The thought was one more source of distress for her.

She needed to get out and do something that would take her mind off this useless worrying. The only person she had spent any pleasurable time with was Dimitri, on the night she met him. Although he had promised to call her, so far that call hadn't come.

The phone rang upstairs and her stomach fluttered in excitement. Could it be Dimitri? Don't be silly, she cautioned herself. If he were going to call, he would have done that by now.

It rang a second time. Should she answer it? It was only three o'clock so she was sure Rosa wasn't home yet. One of the first English lessons Rosa had given her was how to answer the telephone. She'd practiced her "hello' and it passed Rosa's muster, but what if the caller wanted to leave a message? She would never be able to take a message down on paper. It was best to let it ring.

But what if it was Dimitri? She thought he meant it when he said he'd like to call her. Well, she decided, there's only one way to find out. She opened the door to the basement apartment and took the stairs to the main floor two at a time. Out of breath, but full of resolve, she picked up the receiver.

"Hal-lo." It was her best English.

"Hello, may I please speak to Miss Sepsik?"

It was Dimitri! Her breath left her lungs with a soft explosion as she gasped in Ukrainian, "Hello! It's me, Sonja!" He had finally called!

"Would you be able to get away this afternoon? I'm going to pay a visit to an old Ukrainian fellow

116

who's been in Winnipeg for years. You mentioned you might have a relative in Canada. Who knows, he may know something about him."

They made arrangements to meet on Main Street, in front of City Hall, around four o'clock. Then Sonja called Rosa on her cell phone to get permission to go out for the afternoon and evening. Once again, Rosa sounded distracted. She snapped, "Oh, just go, for God's sake!"

As Dimitri hung up the phone he felt some regret that his invitation to Sonja was made, in part, to have her along as his cover. Cover or not, it was the perfect excuse to invite her out. He had enjoyed their brief encounter and sensed she could use a friend. Once more his conscience was at war with his sense of duty; he had never felt comfortable using any and every means possible to get his information. On the one hand he was attracted to Sonja, but on the other hand, he would be using her as a pipeline to the Sinclair home.

It was only a short walk to City Hall from his grubby rooming house so he took his time as he strolled down Main Street. His steps quickened as he entered the underpass below the CPR rail line. It was as much an emotional barrier as a physical barrier between the older north end of the city and downtown.

Gang graffiti adorned the walls of the dank underpass, some overlaid with the creative work of rival gangs. The groups who painted graffiti were usually small street gangs sending coded messages, taunts and challenges in an ongoing war fought for no clear reason and little honour. Although these smaller gangs were a pain in the ass to the local police department, it was the large gangs vying for turf that sucked up the force's manpower. The newspaper had reported seven gang related shootings in the past week, more than enough to keep the police hopping.

Dimitri arrived early at City Hall and took a seat on one of the wooden benches in the small plaza fronting the building. Several strategically grouped flower planters softened the otherwise barren concrete area.

He'd be playing this visit to the old Ukrainian by ear. So much of undercover work was like that. Sift through the mountains of information, and then sift some more until you found the one bright jewel, the one piece that opened more doors and took you forward.

It was only a short while before a bus hissed to a stop at the curb and Sonja stepped onto the sidewalk, eyes shining with pleasure and a wide smile on her face. He rose to meet her and silently cursed the circumstances of their meeting. She had been used so often, and he was yet another user.

"Sonja!" he greeted her in her language. "If I were a poet I would pick one of these flowers and tell you they pale when compared to your beauty." A short bright-yellow skirt bordered in white set off her simple white blouse. Dimitri didn't feel his compliment was an exaggeration.

She threw her head back and laughed. "Dimitri, are you sure you're a deck hand and not some Ukrainian professor of literature in disguise?"

He mentally kicked himself for giving in to flirtation. For one moment he had allowed himself to be a man meeting a pretty woman for a date. That

118

kind of lapse could prove dangerous. He turned his steps eastward toward Jarvis Street, Sonja at his side.

"Apparently this old fellow has been in Winnipeg for years and knows almost every Ukrainian in the city. I hope he'll be able to get me a job." He couldn't let her know he'd already been to the apartment. "I'm not sure of the address but there's a teacup reader living on the main floor so keep your eyes open for her sign."

As they walked he felt the heat of her at his side and savoured the pleasure of it. He fought the urge to take her hand. If she ever learned who he really was, the insult would be compounded if she thought he had also played with her emotions.

The two-story building wasn't difficult to locate, thanks to the garish sign nailed to the wall beside the entrance. The door stood open to a short, filthy hallway with a stairway to the second floor located at the back. Broken mailboxes on one wall bulged with old flyers and discarded trash. The air was foul, awash in the smell of burned meals, urine, and wet laundry, the odours of poverty and neglect.

As Dimitri strained to read the faded lettering on the mailboxes, a door to the side of the cubicles opened to reveal a middle-aged woman with impossibly black hair. The apparition was swathed in a voluminous dressing gown, and a smouldering cigarette dangled from fingers tipped with deep violet polish.

She struck a pose against the door jam and addressed them in a husky voice. "Are ya' looking for an apartment to rent, darlings?"

"No. We're looking for Taras Podricki," Dimitri answered, taken aback by the figure before them. In a vain attempt to conceal her fading beauty, the teacup reader had tried to powder and paint away the lines of excess etched on her full face. It looked as though she had applied her violet lipstick quickly when she heard them enter the building, for in several places it escaped the outline of her lips. For all that, her sultry manner suited the dazzling colours of the tropical flowers and parrots decorating her gown. Dimitri fought to control a smile as he saw the look of surprise on Sonja's face.

"Old Podricki! Well, ya'll have to wait. I heard him go out earlier but he should be back soon. He works the evening shift at the lab so he'll want to get himself some supper before he leaves." With a broad sweep of her large arm she indicated her room. "Come on in! Tell ya' what! I'll read your fortunes for ya' while ya' wait. Little lovebirds like you, it'd be a pleasure to see your future. Miranda will reveal all."

She ushered them into a shabby sitting room where dust motes danced in the sneaky rays of sunlight that somehow found their way through the grimy front windows. The only piece of furniture that looked solid enough to sit on was the old swaybacked sofa; Sonja and Dimitri seated themselves while the woman tended to a kettle and preparations for a pot of tea.

"Say, wha'd ya' want with that old blowhard, anyway?"

"We're from Ukraine, and Sonja was hoping Taras might know one of her relatives who could be living in Winnipeg. He quickly translated the

120

conversation to Sonja while Miranda poured the water into the teapot and set it to steep. Then, for the sake of his cover story, he appeared to be flustered. "I'm sorry, Miranda. Your price for a reading . . . it's probably too expensive for us. I don't have a job yet . . ."

Her laugh rose from deep within and came out full throated, but ended with a smoker's cough. "Damn cigarettes!" She stubbed out the butt in a full ashtray and set it aside. "Aah, don't worry about it. Enjoy the tea. Ya've come to the right place if ya' want info on some Uke relative. Taras and I, we get together once in a while for a sociable drink, and I tell ya', he knows everyone in the community."

A pack of cigarettes materialized from the folds of the dressing gown. She drew one out, hunted for a lighter, and once satisfied it was lit, sat down in a chair that creaked in protest. "That guy, I tell ya'. He can spin a yarn once he's tipped back a few! Likes to pretend he's some kinda' millionaire in disguise. Talks of hidden treasure. I mean, what a load a' bullshit, eh? As if he'd be livin' in this dump if he had some kinda treasure from the old country!" With a dismissive wave of her hand she rose and poured tea into three cheap water glasses.

Once more Dimitri translated the conversation for Sonja. With some pride, she told him she was able to follow what was being said but was happy to hear it repeated in Ukrainian to be sure she understood it correctly.

"Is he a drinking man then?" he asked Miranda as she handed them each a glass.

"Naw, he's a decent hard working guy. Why he's working, I don't know. Should a' been retired a

121

long time ago. Thinks pretty highly of himself though, a real braggart. Brags about having access to places in that lab where he works that a lot of employees don't even have access to. A load of nonsense if ya' ask me!" She blew hard on the hot liquid to cool it and took a loud slurp. "I think his imagination runs away with him. In one breath he goes on about persecution and in another he says he ruined his family."

"He sounds like a man with an active imagination. Does he happen to mention how he ruined them?"

"Naw. The old fool just likes to exaggerate to boost his ego. How'd you like that tea?"

It was a fragrant brew with a thick, almost tarry taste. Dimitri tried to hide his startled reaction when he tasted it, but Miranda hooted with pleasure.

"Lapsang Souchong! It's from China."

The sound of someone entering the building saved them from having to finish their drinks. Miranda looked into the hallway and nodded her head at Dimitri. Taras Podricki was home.

CHAPTER TWELVE

A grey-haired man stood at the mailboxes with his back to Dimitri and Sonja. Two plastic bags of groceries from the local IGA slumped on the floor at his feet.

"Forgive me, vuiko, are you Taras Podricki?" Dimitri asked.

In this neighbourhood, a question such as this would normally elicit a reply such as, "It's none of your business who I am,' but the Ukrainian form of address, vuiko, or uncle, seemed to disarm Taras.

He was not a tall man, although his rigid bearing and the military set of his shoulders gave the illusion of more height than he possessed. His features were coarse, jowly, and he was beginning to develop a paunch, a man long past his prime.

"Who are you? What do you want?" A faint sense of alarm stirred in his wary eyes.

"We're Ukrainians, like you. May we speak with you upstairs, uncle?"

Podricki mumbled a faint, "Come on up," and started up the creaky wooden risers. An enormous grey cat waited by one of the three doors on the landing at the top. At the sound of their steps the monster rose, waved its huge plume-like tail and squalled a coarse greeting.

"Ah, Mitska," Taras addressed the cat. "I have come home with both our suppers." The animal wound itself around the man's legs, then rose up and pawed at his thigh while he juggled the groceries into one hand and fished in his pocket for the door key. What emerged was not a single key but a large ring, heavy with keys of various sizes. From long practice he quickly found the two that fit the dual locks on the old door. The hinges emitted a high-pitched squeal as the door swung open. The neighbourhood, the building, the man, all were neglected but, though beaten down, Dimitri was sure they were not broken.

The cat shot through the door as it opened and disappeared into a small area at the back of the spartan room. As they entered the room, the heat of the day and the stale air trapped within hit Dimitri full force. He was surprised at how tidy the room was: no dirty dishes on the table, no mess of scattered clothes, no unmade bed. Near the window, the latest copy of a local paper, The Ukrainian Voice, lay folded on an overstuffed armchair where the reader would get the best natural light.

Taras waved them to the chairs around the table while he tended to the complaining cat's meal, then he joined them. "Now, tell me what it is you want."

Dimitri cleared his throat. The old man appeared to be very sharp. Would he buy the story? "We are both from Ukraine, near Kiev, and we're told that there's no one in Winnipeg who knows the Ukrainian community better than you do. Perhaps you know someone who is looking for a good worker? I've been here a while and it's difficult, you know . . . my English is okay, but . . ." He left the thought hanging and then quickly changed to another topic. "And we're looking for information about relatives that might possibly be living in Winnipeg. I'm curious to know if I have a cousin here. His name is Vladimir Bolenko."

"Bolenko . . . Bolenko . . ." Taras frowned in concentration as his hand rose to scratch his untidy head of hair. He mulled over the name, rolling it round in his mouth as his mind seemed to sort through, then discard, image after image. "Hmm, Bolenko . . . the name is a common one in the Ukrainian community. Was he from Kiev?"

Dimitri nodded.

"I'm sorry, my friend, the name Vladimir Bolenko does not ring any bells. And your story?" He jutted his chin in Sonja's direction.

"I'm looking for an uncle. His name is, Fjodor Podrinski."

"Similar to yours, isn't it?" Dimitri queried.

The old man's eyes narrowed in suspicion. "My name is very common and has many variations. I'll talk to Father Kostenko. Maybe there is something in the old parish books."

Catching sight of The Ukrainian Voice, Sonja stood and gave a cry of delight. "May I have a look? It's been so long since I've read a newspaper in my language."

Taras glanced at his watch, hesitated, then nodded.

She hurried over to the armchair and grabbed the thin newspaper. Both men smiled at her obvious joy. She settled into the chair by the window and was immediately lost in the pages.

The talk turned to other things and Taras seemed to relax. He lit a cigarette and offered one to Dimitri, who turned it down. How to keep the man talking? He would want to prepare his meal soon and leave for his shift. "I wouldn't normally ask you, but Sonja is into that newspaper and seems to be reading everything from the headlines to the births and deaths columns. Could I bother you for a glass of water?" At the sound of her name Sonja raised her head.

"Of course! It's so hot in here. I apologize. That old hag downstairs probably forced some of her horse piss on you while you waited! I enjoy one beer before supper . . . to get the digestion going. Would you join me? And you Sonja?"

He hurried to the kitchen and to Dimitri's surprise, returned with three cold Slavutich Ukrainian Pilsners. Dimitri didn't have to feign enjoyment as he savoured his first mouthful.

Taras was a man who lived alone, and now he had an audience. He began to talk and Dimitri steered him to his job at the lab. Sonja quickly lost interest and was once more immersed in the paper.

"We're three night employees in my block. One security guard and two janitors. Well, not just janitors really." He added with a note of pride, "It's more than just emptying trash cans, you know. Plus," he added, and appeared to swell with self-importance, "once a week I cart the specimens that need to be disposed of over to P-Block, where liquid and solid waste is rendered and sterilized. That's a job, I'll tell you! Just learning Section D2"The Hazardous Waste Disposal Protocol, was a chore. There's a state-of-the-art sterilizer down there that renders the tissue into sludge and uses high-pressure autoclaves and paddles to kill any germ you can name. You have no idea what amazing machines these labs have nowadays." His eyes shone with pleasure.

Taras was on a roll and Dimitri felt that the best way to keep him talking was to challenge him.

"Sure I have! My sister-in-law, in Kiev, is a lab technician."

"Bah! You can't compare our modern facility with a lab in Russia!"

"Don't underestimate Russian science. Anyway, Kiev is in Ukraine."

"Russian science, huh!" Taras almost spit with contempt. "Science like Chernobyl, maybe? Here, look at this." He hauled a scrapbook out from a closet near the bed. It was full of old photos, scraps of paper, and notices from both The Ukrainian Voice and The Winnipeg Free Press. He flipped to the back pages and proudly displayed articles relating to the lab and some of the machinery purchases. "Here's good technology. The labs in Ukraine could only hope to have machines such as these. Here, look! Here's the tissue sterilizer, and here's the wastewater sterilizer. This is high-tech equipment, I tell you!"

The hint of an idea took shape in Dimitri's mind. The man wanted to be affirmed in his job, acknowledged for what he did. "I don't see anything so fantastic about that machine. It just looks like a stainless steel drum to me."

"Simple! Simple, you say? It took . . . Well, I tell you what! You need a job, yes? It's Sundays that I move the tissue to P-Block. Maybe you can help me out next Sunday? Then I can show you the difference in technology between the East and the West."

A way into the lab! Dimitri found it difficult to keep a look of triumph off his face.

127

As Taras closed the book several old photos slid to the floor. He stooped to gather them up but as he reached for one of them his hands stilled. It was a group photo, possibly from the 1920s, a formal shot done in a photographer's studio. An older couple sat in the front row, a young child on the woman's lap. Behind them stood the couple's other children. Taras gazed long at the photo, then raised his head and stared across the room to where Sonja sat. Was he looking at Sonja or was he seeing through the window to a moment in the past that the photo evoked? A range of emotions crossed the old man's face, but they were gone before Dimitri had a chance to read them.

At that moment Sonja closed the newspaper and laid it aside. The action seemed to interrupt Taras' thoughts and he quickly shoved the picture into the scrapbook and pushed the whole thing under the sagging sofa.

"Have you worked at the lab for a long time Mr. Podricki?" Sonja asked as she re-joined them.

Dimitri thought Taras appeared distracted, as though he found it hard to gather his thoughts. Something happened. But what? It was something to do with the photo.

"The lab? Oh, no, not long," Taras replied to Sonja's question. "I was a gardener for many years." Once again his need to boast surfaced and he flushed with pride. "I worked for many important families, the Evanthorpes, the Sinclairs, the Maynes." His eyes never left her face. Searching, searching. They probed the angles, the shape of the chin, searching.

"The Sinclairs? James Sinclair's? I work there too. I'm . . . well, right now I'm a housekeeper." Hot spots of shame flamed on her cheeks but the older man seemed to miss her discomfort.

"You live at the house! Such a coincidence. Mr. Sinclair asked me to come and trim his shrubs on Saturday, so I am making a special trip to the house. Perhaps I could bring you the new copy of The Ukrainian Voice. It comes out on Friday."

Taras' mind was obviously no longer on machines or the lab, but Dimitri quickly pinned down a time to join him on Sunday at the building. The guard was a friend, Taras said. They often fished together. He felt sure there would be no problem getting Dimitri inside to help with the extra burden of the Sunday work schedule.

They made their goodbyes and left the building for the welcome, cooler air of the street. Dimitri turned their steps south, towards downtown, but Sonja took his hand to stop him.

"I'm sorry if I was rude in there. When I saw that Ukrainian paper I forgot everything else. It's been such a long time since I've had a chance to read a newspaper""

He halted her apology with a smile. "You weren't rude. He didn't know anything about your uncle anyway. And as far as a job for me," he shrugged his shoulders as they resumed their walk. "We'll see about that after Sunday." They were still holding hands and it felt natural.

It was after six o'clock and well into the supper hour. Dimitri had asked Sonja to get the afternoon and evening off so she would assume he was going to provide her with supper. He quickly ran over his finances before making a suggestion about their meal.

"I'm sorry Sonja, but I don't have much money to spend on our supper. We could order one of those large bowls of soup in Chinatown, the ones with pieces of chicken or pork in them."

Her laugh chased away any lingering thoughts about his undercover work. Sonja slipped her arm through his and quickened her steps. "I love that soup! And I have a little of my own money. We can even order two egg rolls. I can taste them already!"

CHAPTER THIRTEEN

Ralf Altmann slouched in his chair, weak from the heat of a Miami summer afternoon. The shade of a large, poolside umbrella did little to combat the blanket of humidity that weighed him down. He was exhausted. Damn Panamanian. Just because he can take the heat doesn't mean we all have to golf in the middle of the afternoon. The focus of his anger was Juan Maria Alvarz del Valdes, known to those with more than a passing acquaintance as Juan.

Juan was a financial genius, as well as a citizen of a country with lax money laws. As a result, he occupied a high position within the organization. If Juan wanted to play a round of golf during the Miami quarterly conference, then everyone golfed. While Altmann had no problem with the game itself, he felt there were better times to play eighteen holes than in the stifling heat of the afternoon.

Early mornings in Miami were usually cool and clear, much more conducive to an enjoyable game.

Juan took care of the organization's dirty money by washing it through legitimate businesses in various European cities. Rumours of his unpredictable Latin temper, and the dubious quality of some of his friendships, insulated him from petty grumbling about high temperatures and a slick, sweaty grip on a five iron.

As though summoned by Altmann's unhappy, heat-laden thoughts, Juan strolled out of the mansion onto the patio, a drink in his hand. The man's slim physique and dark features meant he looked good in anything he chose to wear, but especially the white pants and shirt he'd changed into. To Ralf's continued annoyance, Juan appeared untouched by the wilting temperatures.

"Tell me, Ralf. How's that problem in your district? With Sinclair. Can I expect a drop in revenue over the next little while?" As he spoke, he rattled the ice cubes in the glass he held.

"Because of his wife's prying? I don't think so. In a couple of days she won't be in a position to cause problems."

The elegant arching of a dark eyebrow prompted Altmann to explain.

"Since the problem came from his own household, I told him to take care of it, personally. We'll have proof of his loyalty, as well as a guarantee that he won't develop remorse over her death and shoot off his mouth to the local authorities. As a last consideration, it saves us the cost of a contract hit."

Silence. The silence lengthened and spoke volumes about Juan's opinion of the way the situation had been handled. Altmann shivered as sweat traced a path down his spine and soaked the waistband of his pants. How stupid could he be? He should have consulted with Miami first before giving Sinclair the order! The slim Latin face before him retained a neutral expression but the eyes darkened in anger. Altmann tightened his sphincter muscles and cursed the foolishness of his actions.

"Have you any idea what you've done?" Juan's tone was controlled, too controlled. He slid into a chair and adjusted the meticulous creases in his pants. "What if he's charged with the murder?"

"He has the perfect scapegoat. His gardener is a former Nazi with a grudge against the Sinclair woman. He can easily be framed." The explanation sounded weak, inept, even to Ralf's own ears.

"We all have a stake in each other's actions. Anything that happens in your jurisdiction affects the organization as a whole. Did you talk this over with our legal counsel before having your chat with Sinclair?"

"It seemed straightforward to me. I was told to take care of it and""

"Bastante . . . enough!" Juan rose from his seat, stiff with anger. "Come. We need to meet with Pavel."

***

"So you come to me now like I'm some kind of God damned genie that you pull out of a bottle! You think I can fix everything for you?" The lawyer sat amid a sea of papers destined to be handouts at the evening meeting. In the corner next to a photocopier, a shredder capable of turning a sheet of paper into confetti awaited its nightly feed of material too sensitive to leave the house. "If you'd come to me before setting your little plan in action I would've reminded you of plea bargaining, and the Witness Protection Program. Nobody's naive enough to think the RCMP doesn't know that Sinclair's knee deep into something."

"Look, we've got the crime lab in our pocket. Laury O'Connor can make sure the crime samples clear Sinclair before he's charged with anything. I'm quite confident we can get rid of the threat Sinclair's

133

wife poses, and tighten our grip on Sinclair this way."

Juan's silence since they'd entered the room went a long way to giving Altmann his confidence back. The Panamanian stood by the window deep in thought, his slim hands clasped loosely behind his back. He turned now and addressed the two men.

"One way or another, my friends, Sinclair is now a weak link in our chain. If we have him take care of his wife he might have second thoughts, and, as you point out, Pavel, there's the chance he could clear his conscience with a plea bargain. On the other hand, if we have one of our own contacts remove Mrs. Sinclair, we face the same risk. He could panic, break under pressure."

Altmann saw where Juan's train of thought was headed and felt relief. No matter how it played out, James Sinclair was a dead man. He just didn't know it yet. Ralf Altmann, on the other hand, could pick himself out of the near mess he'd made of the problem. Eager to get off the hook, he took over the narrative.

"So, it doesn't matter if Sinclair's a suspect, or not. Either way, he's got to go, and fast, before the investigation starts to dig too deep. With both of them out of the picture it'll read like the bikers got tired of sharing the turf and eliminated the competition. It means we'd have to call someone in from Chicago, though."

Juan circled the littered room, a finger toying with his lower lip. "That leaves us with a vacuum in Winnipeg. And a loss of revenue for a while. Not good. I like what I've heard about this guy . . . this Laury O'Connor. The way he's been handling the organ sales is impressive. Very impressive indeed. And of course his position in the lab is invaluable."

As he passed the desk where the lawyer sat, he stopped and regarded the man. "You're being very quiet, Counsellor. Do you have something you wish to add to the subject?"

The lawyer spread his hands in a helpless gesture and shook his head. "I'm just glad this room is swept for bugs twice a day. Leave me out of it. The three of us won't settle something like this anyway. That's what these quarterly meetings are for. I suggest you add it to the agenda."

"True. Ralf, let's take a walk on the beach. We'll enjoy the view while you fill me in, give me some background information. If we put our heads together, maybe come up with a plan of action, it will save a lot of time later."

Altmann nodded his assent but groaned inwardly. The sun's rays still packed a wallop and he didn't relish a stroll in the sand. Did the guy never break into a sweat?

CHAPTER FOURTEEN

A small apartment on the top floor of a three-story walk up served as the cover team's safe-house. Sparsely furnished, it contained only the items necessary for the team to meet and debrief. Occasionally, a nervous trial witness spent a few days housed in the apartment for his or her own safety and a poignant poem scrawled on the wall above the bed testified to the mental turmoil the rooms had witnessed:

"Now Trevor's gone and I'm alone.

Who will come to take ME home?"

The writer may have found some measure of shelter within the walls, but Dimitri was sure it was fleeting and cold. Few who were caught up in the justice system had someone, as Trevor apparently did, who cared enough to search them out and take them home.

When Dimitri let himself in, the sight of a six-pack of beer and a box of pizza on the coffee table greeted him. Rudy Savage balanced an oozing piece of deep-dish pepperoni on the fingers of one hand while he struggled with the pull-tab on a can of beer with the other.

"Good timing, Stan. You're just in time to save me from death by dehydration. I tell ya', man should have' been born with three hands."

Stan felt a jolt of pleasure at being addressed by his real name. It felt good, even for a little while, to set aside all artifice and be himself. He pulled the beer tab for Rudy and received muffled thanks through a mouthful of pizza.

"Any chance there's a 7-Up around? I've seen enough beer over the last couple months to last a lifetime."

"Will Coke do? Kinda figured you might be turning off beer. It's in the fridge."

The sagging sofa, while not especially inviting, offered one of the best seats in the room. Stan settled into it and worked his feet onto the littered coffee table. While they ate, he filled Rudy in on recent events, including the details of his beating and his meeting with Sonja.

"So what's the news on your end of the investigation?" he asked, after Rudy finished giving his faded bruises a good looking over.

"I'm here to give you the old "good news-bad news" routine. The good news is that CISC has finally opened up a bit and given us some information that could apply to this case."

Stan licked the last of the pizza grease from his fingers, then fished through the jumble on the small table for a napkin to finish the job. "That's good news. Things aren't exactly happening fast around here. Of course, that could change come Sunday if I get into the lab. What's the bad news?"

"The bad news is the good news, if you catch my drift. The FBI has tipped CISC that there's a contract out on a big shot businessman here. No names. No more information. We know of only a few men in Winnipeg who would qualify for a hit. Our bet's on Sinclair."

Stan's hands stilled as he took in the news. "He must have pissed someone off big time to warrant a hit. Any idea why?"

"Sorry. We're coming up empty on it. No sign of missteps on the part of old man Sinclair. Now, his wife . . ." Rudy exhaled through pursed lips. "Well, that's another story. She's got everyone pissed off at her. Immigration knows, although they can't prove anything, that she's pulling a scam by bringing in girls. There's a regular turf war brewing between her and the bikers. And to top it off, there're hints she's nosing around for information on the head of the lab, Laury O'Connor. One of her girls likes to chat a bit too much. Says that Rosa wants to get dealt into the game that James and Laury O'Connor have going."

"There's a definite tie-in with Sinclair and the lab all right. I caught a shift this week with his trucking firm. Hung around the dispatch area making a nuisance of myself until they put me on with a driver whose swamper didn't show up. Anyway, he's telling me how the trucking company's in for a lawsuit because Sinclair ordered a shipment of goldeye bumped. Replaced the space with a cooler from the lab. The fish sat in the warehouse overnight and ended up bad by the time it arrived in France. Must've been something pretty important in that cooler to risk a lawsuit."

Rudy popped the tab on another beer before he answered. "Well, wouldn't a medical shipment take priority over a shipment of gourmet fish?"

"Yah, sure. But here's the thing. It was a cooler. That means whatever it held was perishable. The lab deals in samples, dead stuff. Sure, in the virology section it deals with live viruses, but they're handled in a totally different way. They're triple packed and clearly marked with an infectious agent label. And they're packed with dry ice.

I've got a feeling that cooler held a live organ. That's what I'm going to be looking for when I get into the lab on Sunday, evidence that they're trafficking in organs."

Rudy's hand made a slow descent and his beer can came to rest on the table. "Organ trafficking," he stated solemnly as he nodded. "That's something Sinclair would be in on, for sure. Good work there, buddy." He scooped his beer from the table and saluted Stan before taking a deep swallow.

"Okay," Stan said as he held up his fingers to tick off items as he spoke. "What've we got? Number one, we've got Sinclair's missus tied into running prostitutes and importing girls to fill her massage parlours. She's having a bit of trouble with the bikers because of territory. Number two, we've got a likely link between Sinclair and the lab, possibly organ trafficking, although at this stage that's just a suspicion. Number three, we've got information on a hit being planned on a Winnipeg big shot. Again, just a suspicion, but a good possibility that it's Sinclair. And, number four, we've got Sinclair doing some hush-hush dealings with suspected members of the Ukrainian mafia. They would be the ones who broker the deals for the organs on the other end."

"It's tempting to let things ride for a while and let Sinclair get taken down. Winnipeg would be a better place without him." Rudy paused for a moment to suck at a tooth, an action Stan recognized as a sign the older man had given his next words a lot of thought. "Ya' know, man's a funny creature. He's never satisfied with what he's got. Take Sinclair now. He's got a couple of good legitimate businesses, there's no way of telling how much he's got socked away in some Swiss Bank, and still the guy wants more. How much can you spend in one lifetime? Know what I mean?"

Stan grunted in agreement, then was silent for a moment as he considered his answer. Despite Rudy's rough exterior, Stan had realized early in their partnership that the man was a deep thinker. "Maybe it's just a matter of balance," he said.

The questioning look on Rudy's face prompted Stan to continue. "This hunger for more, faster, better, whatever it is that drives us. Maybe it's what's raised us up from the cave man era. If we'd been content with the way things were, well, we wouldn't have tried to make our existence better, would we? We'd still be mucking around in stinking caves."

A smile tugged at the corners of his friend's mouth. "Well, I'll be damned! We've got ourselves a philosopher." He reached over and gave Stan a light punch on the shoulder. "Can't say I disagree with ya'. It's just too damn bad some of us otherwise smart creatures let that desire turn into a passion. Then we're going down a road we're better off not traveling."

Stan grinned and brought the conversation back to the original topic. "As far as Sinclair goes . . . well, he's still a citizen of this country and, like it or not, we're sworn to protect him. If we can prevent this hit from going down, then that's what we're going to do. But I'm also going to do my best to send the bastard away for a very long time."

An hour later, Stan left the apartment, crammed his baseball cap on his head, and was once more under cover as Dimitri Bolenko.

CHAPTER FIFTEEN

Saturday morning, and the empty hours of the day stretched before Sonja with the promise of nothing but boredom. Like a trapped animal, she paced her small basement apartment, from bedroom to sitting room and back to the bedroom. She knew every inch of the place and with each day she grew to hate it more. As much as she loathed the thought, she was almost beginning to think it would be a relief when Rosa sent her to work.

The heat of the past few weeks had cooled overnight to a more comfortable temperature and the day was too perfect to waste staying inside. She'd take a walk before lunch. The exercise would do her good, and it would get her out of the house. Rosa and James were both home this morning, and Sonja knew they would be at each other's throats as soon as Rosa got out of bed. The tension in the house these past few days had been almost unbearable.

Better yet, I'll pack a sandwich and a piece of fruit and walk to the park to eat lunch. I'll take a magazine. And I'll force myself to read it from cover to cover before I come home. One way or another I'll learn English and get out of here.

As she rummaged in the fridge for ingredients to make a sandwich, a sound caught her attention. Fftt, fftt, fftt. That's odd. That's the sprinklers. But they're supposed to go on at night. Should she go out to investigate a possible malfunction? On her way to the back door she passed the kitchen window that overlooked the pool area and the garden shed. A movement near the back of the shed caught her eye. James emerged from the shrubbery that concealed the sprinkler controls. He was aware of the problem then. Good. He could take care of it.

Within minutes, she had a ham sandwich packed in a paper bag, along with some grapes, and a bottle of iced tea. All she needed was a magazine and she'd be on her way. There was one that had caught her attention a few days ago in the living room.

To reach the living room from the kitchen, Sonja had to pass a hallway that led to the bedrooms. As she made her way across the narrow passage the sound of angry voices, a man's and a woman's, echoed down the hall from the direction of the master bedroom. James must have come in the side door, or through the bedroom's small patio doors. It was unusual for Rosa to be awake before noon on Saturday, and if James came in and woke her" well, that would be enough to start an argument.

Sonja quickly made her way to the living room, snatched the magazine from the coffee table and left by the front door.

The sprinklers in the front yard blasted water at full force. Normally the water sprayed in a gentle mist, but now the walkway, flowerbeds and shrubs were drenched. Obviously, James hadn't been able to fix the problem. As Sonja waited for the heavy jet of water to pass over the sidewalk, she heard the thud of water as it hit the windows around the side of the house.

I should go back and make sure all the windows are closed. No, I don't want to run into either James or Rosa, especially if they're in a foul mood. I'll check them from the outside.

She set her bag on the dry area near the door and sprinted around the side of the house, timing her run to avoid the oscillating jet of cold water. The windows were closed, but in the process of checking, she'd muddied her shoes in a flowerbed. She would clean them later, but for now she could go on her walk without worrying about the bedrooms getting wet.

At the foot of the long curving drive she turned right toward the river and the large park that ran along its shore. With each step that carried her away from the Sinclair house her mood lightened. The soft morning breeze held the sharp smell of freshly cut grass, and in the distance she heard the sound of children's laughter. It was a perfect day. She resolved to put everything from her mind that might ruin it.

As she reached the end of the second block, a small red squirrel shot across the sidewalk and vanished up the backside of an elm that overhung the intersection. From the safety of a high limb, he scolded her for invading his territory. "You have a brave voice for such a small creature," she called to the angry bundle of fur.

"He is unhappy with you, Sonja. Have you offended him?"

The voice came from directly behind her. With a gasp of surprise, she whirled around to confront the speaker and instinctively raised her fist to protect herself.

"I'm so sorry I frightened you, my dear." Taras Podricki was dressed in coveralls and carried a wide brimmed hat in one hand. He had a small duffel bag in the other.

Sonja let out her breath with a small self-conscious laugh. "Oh, Mr. Podricki, you scared me." It was only then that she remembered their conversation earlier in the week. He had mentioned he was coming to trim the Sinclairs' hedges and would bring her a copy of The Ukrainian Voice newspaper. She'd almost missed his visit.

"Please, I would prefer if you called me Taras, or perhaps Uncle Taras, as we do in the old country." He smiled sadly. "I really didn't intend to surprise you. I got off the bus, just down the block." He pointed out the tall blue pole marking the bus stop.

She felt comfortable with this man and would have no problem calling him Uncle Taras. "My mother used to say that a good scare once in a while was good for the heart."

"Aah, yes. I believe she would have said, "A good scare reminds the heart it's alive.'"

"That's it! But how did you know? Is it such a common expression in Ukraine?"

"No, but it was an expression that was used a lot in my family. I have something to show you child, and we have much to discuss. You were on your way to do an errand perhaps? Am I keeping you from something?"

She indicated the bag that contained her lunch. "No, not at all. Actually, I was on my way to the park to have my lunch and read a magazine. The lawn sprinklers are on at the Sinclairs anyway, so

145

you can't do the hedges right now. Should we go over to the park together? Find a table that's private? We can talk there if you'd like."

"Excellent. What we have to discuss is best done without prying ears. Lead the way, my dear."

Sonja allowed the older man to set the pace as they made their way along the sidewalk, one minute walking in a pool of sunlight, the next in the deep shade of one of the magnificent elms that bordered the street. Although she burned with curiosity, she held her questions in check as they covered the final three blocks to the park. He must have found her uncle, or at least some news of him. Perhaps she wasn't alone in the city after all.

The park was huge, and even though it was Saturday, they were able to find a vacant table near a clump of silver dogwoods. In a gallant gesture reminiscent of gentler times, Uncle Taras dusted the seat for Sonja with the edge of the newspaper, then placed his hat on the table and sat down across from her. After a moment's hesitation, he drew an old photo out of the pocket of his coveralls and laid it on the table, keeping it covered with his hand.

"Do you recognize this photo, Sonja?" he asked, removing his hand from the sepia toned portrait.

Her shock brought goosebumps to her arms. With a cry of delight, she reached for the photo and gently ran her fingers over the worn surface. "It's my mother's family! See, there. That girl? That's my mother. That's my grandfather and grandmother. And that baby? That's my uncle Fjodor. I never met him and my mother didn't talk much about him. But how did you get this? Is he here in Winnipeg?"

The last time she'd seen the picture was when she moved into the smaller apartment after her mother died. Just before leaving Ushgorod she had mailed one small packet of photos and family records to her brother for safekeeping, but this photo hadn't been precious enough for her to rescue. "I don't understand," she said. "Where did you"" She stopped when she saw the pain on the old man's face.

"That is also a picture of my family, Sonja. That is my mother and father. That little girl is my sister. My name is not Taras Podricki."

Time stood still. Birds still called in the trees and the children still yelled to each other as they kicked a soccer ball through the grass, but the sounds seemed far away. Sonja's senses narrowed to focus on the table and the grey-haired man seated across from her. She drew her finger along the edge of the photo, and as her nail passed over the tattered edge the rasping sound it produced magnified, then swelled to fill her ears. She willed herself to breathe, fought to allow her stunned mind to accept the words this man had spoken. Her eyes followed the path of a small insect as it traveled along the gap between the boards of the table. This man claimed to be her uncle, the mysterious black sheep of the family that her father had despised.

Taras watched the swift progression of emotions across the face of the girl seated in front of him: shock, disbelief, denial, suspicion. She was so much like his sister, Aniko, slow to accept a stranger, but fiercely loyal to her family. How would Sonja see him? As a stranger, or as her uncle? Was he doing the right thing by opening up

147

to the girl? And if she accepted him, what then? What could he offer her? He was family, and willing to accept his role as her uncle. But as well as family ties, he would bring dark secrets to the relationship. Secrets that had divided the family in the past. Secrets that drove him out of his homeland and still held him in their grip today.

He was old now. He needed family around him for whatever time he had left. And perhaps he would take the secrets to his grave rather than pass their heavy burden to the next generation.

Sonja's voice, when she spoke, had a little-girl quality. "Uncle Fjodor?"

148

CHAPTER SIXTEEN

It was true. She knew it was true. She could see it now when she really looked for the similarities. The shape of the head, the curve of the mouth, it was like seeing someone she knew long ago through a flawed glass. This wasn't Taras Podricki; the man seated before her was her mother's brother.

"Uncle Fjodor?" she asked again.

The man's gaze softened and Sonja realized he had been prepared for her to deny a relationship. Or worse yet, prepared for her to get up and walk away.

"I have been Taras for so long now that I couldn't answer to anything else. I would be honoured if you just called me Uncle Taras. I know you've heard many bad things about me." He nodded toward the photo she still held in her hand.

"Not from my mother, but from my father . . . yes. He refused to allow your name spoken in our home. He said you fought with the Nazis."

He avoided her gaze while his fingers shaped and then reshaped the brim of the gardener's hat that lay on the table between them.

"It's true. It's perhaps hard for you, as a young person, to understand how things were before you were born. In my youth I witnessed the cruelty of the Russians against the Ukrainian people. They confiscated the grain the peasants produced, they took their livestock. People starved to death, died of disease or succumbed to the bitter cold because they couldn't afford fuel. Certainly, for many Ukrainians, the Germans were liberators.

"When my best friend lied about his age and joined the German army, he encouraged me to do the same. His grandparents had just died, possibly of old age. But their deaths were hastened by hunger. We were both very young, but big for our age. And we were angry. It didn't take much for him to talk me into it."

He raised his head and looked her squarely in the eye. "For life there is no rehearsal, Sonja. You have one chance at it and if you choose wrong, the consequences are with you always."

Sonja bowed her head to hide her own shame. This was something she knew first hand. Perhaps there was a curse on the family that caused each generation to make poor choices. Was her father's past so free from error that he could judge and condemn this man?

Her uncle continued with his story. "We realized too late that the Nazis were evil." He gave a bitter laugh. "But by then they owned us. We had to wear their uniforms so we were isolated from our fellow Ukrainians in the units; they even tattooed us under the arm, like a brand."

"A tattoo . . . I don't understand . . ."

"They said it was in case we were wounded . . . so they could identify us if we needed blood." He waved away the explanation. "Lies. It was so that we could not desert or change sides. If a soldier was captured by the Russians and they found the tattoo . . ." He didn't continue with the sentence and Sonja didn't press him.

"I'm sorry, Uncle Taras, you must have gone through hell."

"It was hell, Sonja, but any war is hell. In a sense though, I was lucky. Although I went into Russia with the army, I didn't actually have to fight with the troops." The old man's gaze focused on the middle distance over her shoulder, as though he watched the past replayed on a screen only he could see.

"I suppose they could see I was underage, just a child really, but they were in desperate need of recruits. It's been said they took boys as young as twelve. I was assigned as the personal orderly to Obersturmfuhrer Widenmayer, a man totally lacking in what you and I would call human emotion. I served him well, but it was out of fear, not respect."

Although he fell silent, it was apparent to Sonja that the memories played on in his mind.

Finally, he broke with the past and rubbed his hands over his face, as though to scrub the pictures from his eyes. "Enough of these old stories! I have a bad habit of monopolizing the conversation. Please, you must tell me about my sister, and the rest of your family. And tell me how it is that you came to Canada."

Sonja realized that her stories would be no more pleasant than those of her Uncle Fjodor. He knew nothing of her father's disappearance because of his political beliefs, the fate of her brother Misha, or the death of her mother. How to tell him of his namesake, her brother Fjodor, and the degradation she had suffered at his hands after he helped her escape from Ukraine?

151

From the quiet area of their picnic table Sonja looked out over the activity of the park. Mothers chatted together on benches while they kept a careful eye on their young children in the wading pool; a group of teens played a lively game of soccer on the grassy area, while a young couple strolled hand-in-hand along the path by the river.

We sit in the sunshine in this peaceful park and yet we speak of death and betrayal. Life was so different in Ukraine. There wasn't the luxury of carefree times in the park. Thank God we've left it behind us. We'll make a new start here.

"Look, Uncle," she said as she placed her lunch on the picnic table. "I've brought a lunch. It's small, but we'll share it. We have a lot of years to catch up on, and we might as well eat as we talk."

With a light laugh Taras retrieved his duffel bag from the grass at his feet and placed it on the table beside the smaller bag. "And I've brought a lunch as well. We'll mix and match. This will be quite the picnic." He rubbed his hands together briskly, then unzipped his bag.

Sonja began to recapture the sense of freedom she'd felt earlier in the day when she left the Sinclairs.' She would be okay now. She wasn't alone anymore.

***

"Where in the hell have you been, Taras? You were supposed to be here before noon! It's almost two o'clock. I have better things to do with my day than sit around waiting for you to show up and trim my hedges!"

James Sinclair was pacing at the foot of the drive when Sonja and Taras returned to the house.

Now, as he confronted them, he repeatedly ran his hands through his thinning hair, exposing the damp patches of perspiration on the underarms of his polo shirt. He was visibly agitated and furious with his former gardener.

Taras stood mute under the barrage of the verbal assault.

Sonja quickly cut across the still damp grass to make her way to the back door and, she hoped, escape James' scrutiny. It had been hard to explain to her uncle how she'd ended up in Canada, and by the time she'd reached the end of her story she was crying bitter tears. Her eyes still felt hot and swollen, and there was no way she wanted James to question the cause of her crying.

As she entered the house she was once again filled with despair at having to call this place her temporary home. Maybe she could work out some short-term living arrangement with Uncle Taras. His apartment was small, but anything was better than living here.

Thankfully, Rosa was nowhere to be seen. The kitchen was exactly as she'd left it that morning, so no one had eaten lunch. Rosa was probably holed up in her room fuming over the argument with James. From the way James had acted when they came up the drive, they must have had a terrible row.

A small bathroom opened off the back entry, so Sonja didn't bother going downstairs to her basement washroom to splash cold water on her swollen eyes. Through the open window she heard James give directions to Taras about trimming the shrubs. Although he still sounded impatient, his agitation seemed to have decreased somewhat.

"I had a problem with the sprinkler this morning and wasted half an hour getting it turned off, but it looks like everything has dried out enough for you to get in there without getting too wet. Concentrate on the shrubs that grow up against the house. They're really overgrown and I don't like it when they get so tall that they block the light. I've written out a cheque for your wages. I figure it should take you about three hours and I've calculated for that. If it takes longer, give me a call and I'll send you another one for the difference."

Minutes later James stood in the kitchen, shouting for Sonja. If Rosa was indeed sleeping, Sonja thought, he'd wake her for sure.

"Sonja, the barbecue isn't working and I don't have time to get the part I need to fix it. Here's some money. I've written the part number on this paper, and the address for the shop that carries it, it's past the airport in Oak Point. I want you to pick it up for me this afternoon. They're open until four o'clock, so you'll have to leave right now to make it there by bus before they close. Do you understand what I've told you to do?"

Sonja nodded and took the address and money he handed her. She understood his instructions and she also realized it would take her several hours to make the return trip to Oak Point on the bus. Fortunately, he was in such a rush to leave that he hadn't noticed her red eyes.

Downstairs in her basement suite, she retrieved the backpack she used as a purse and put the money and the list in one of the smaller side pockets. On her way out she meant to ask Uncle Taras if he had remembered to bring her The Ukrainian Voice so she could read it on the bus, but he was busy working on the shrubs by the bedroom windows and Sonja didn't bother him. She had his phone number; she would call him tomorrow.

CHAPTER SEVENTEEN

"Somebody, help! Please! My wife . . . she's not breathing. Someone broke in here and killed my wife." The call was logged in at 5:18 pm. A First Response Unit was dispatched and arrived at the Sinclair home at 5:25.

Detective Sergeant Michael Berger of the Major Crimes Division pulled into the long driveway of the Sinclair residence and came to a stop behind three other police vehicles. Shit. The lawn's crawling with cops. What'd they do? Send every goddamned rookie on the force to this call? One spit on the wrong blade of grass and the entire crime scene is contaminated!

"Curious Michael' his mom had called him when he was a kid. He was curious about everything. Why was his favourite word and how wasn't far behind. It was no surprise to anyone who knew him that he went into police work. His first question when he arrived at a crime scene was "How did they do it?' and his next was "Why did they do it?' He had a good record of finding out the answer to both.

He heaved his large body from the car and assessed the situation. It was a given the crime scene was contaminated. The paramedics were here so their hair, fibre and footprints would be all over the scene. Thank God there were ways to weed out some of the compromised evidence.

"Matthews!" he called to a rookie with enough sense to stay on the walkway that led to the house.

The kid had obviously read the handbook on crime scene investigation and taken it to heart. He'd go places in the force if he kept his nose clean. "I want you to take down the plate number of every vehicle on this block, and the ones in this garage." He tossed him the car keys in case they needed to move his vehicle for any reason, then made his way up the flower-lined sidewalk to the front door.

The grass and the soil in the flowerbeds were damp. As it hadn't rained in days, the owners must have used their sprinkler system today. A groan escaped his lips as a woman, possibly a neighbour, came around from the back of the house.

"Get this yard roped off with tape. And make sure no one gets through from the back," he shouted to no one in particular. This one was high profile, he could feel it in his bones, and he'd make sure it was done by the book.

Constable Pelly greeted him at the door and Berger was gratified to see a log book and a pen on an elegant hall table. As he entered his name, he counted eight names on the list. Good, they had limited access to the house. "Anyone in the house not on the list?" he asked.

Pelly nodded. "The husband. He called it in. There's a young woman downstairs, too. Doesn't understand English very well. Says she's Ukrainian and she looks damned scared. I've got an officer with her 'cause I'm afraid she'll run if she's left on her own." His jaws worked rhythmically on a wad of gum.

"Get Klarysa over here, she speaks Ukrainian. If she's not available, ask for Eva. She speaks a couple of those European languages. Which way to the bedroom?" Pelly jerked his thumb over his shoulder indicating the back area of the house. "And Pelly," Berger continued. "Swallow that gum. The last thing we need is to find your DNA in some ashtray."

Pelly reddened and swallowed.

The house felt like a sauna. It didn't make sense that a classy mansion like this didn't have air-conditioning. True, for the past half-hour the doors were constantly being opened as a steady stream of people came and went, and an air-conditioner would have to work hard to keep the temperature down, but he would have expected it to be cooler than it was. He found the thermostat on the wall in the hallway to the master bedroom. It was set for the summer cooling cycle all right, but it was turned off. He made a mental note to have it dusted for prints and to have the photographer get a close up shot of the settings.

It was a large bedroom but with so many people in it, it was crowded. Two paramedics stood off in a corner next to a fragile chair. They'd seen this type of thing before and seemed to know the routine, touch nothing, be ready with answers.

Sergeant Emil Turner greeted Berger, and Berger returned the greeting. "Emil. So, what've we got? Walk me through it."

Turner flipped to the beginning of his notebook. "The husband came home and noticed his wife hadn't gotten up all day. Came in here and found her unresponsive. He called 911 and a First Response Unit arrived a few minutes later. The paramedics couldn't get a response, figure she'd been dead for several hours."

As Berger listened to what Turner had to say, he scanned the room, his glance lingering on the glass strewn carpet.

Turner indicated the garden doors leading to the small patio. "Window over there's been broken, probably from the outside, given the location of the glass inside the room, but we'll check the hackle marks, just to be sure the blow was struck from the outside. The blind was drawn all the way up. We've found a set of footprints under the window and along the flowerbeds. They're a fair size, could be a man's or a large woman's. Another set of prints is considerably smaller, probably a woman's."

He licked the tip of a finger and turned the page before continuing. "The victim has been identified by the husband. Name's Rosa Sinclair. We've got the husband in his home office on the other side of the house and there's a woman downstairs. Could be the maid. She's pretty hysterical. Can't speak much English.

"Medical Examiner just got here. Confirms the death is suspicious but as usual he's keeping mum. That's about it," he concluded as he snapped the notebook shut.

Berger stroked his chin as he continued to eye the layout of the room. His gaze came to rest at the window. He worked his way carefully across the room, stopping occasionally to get a closer look at an item. "Someone must think we're really stupid."

"Pardon?"

"Window's broken from the outside, right? The dirt around that pint-sized patio is damp. Any dirty footprints inside? Any blood on the glass?" A

159

stubby index finger pointed first to the carpet, then to the shattered glass.

"Nope."

"So she does what? Wakes up when someone breaks one of the panes on her door; stays put when they reach in and unlock the door; sits there in bed while some yahoo comes in, without cutting himself; and then she lets him smother her? Make sense to you?"

"Nope. Can't say that it does."

"By the way, has anyone checked that the doors are actually unlocked?"

Turner stepped to the garden doors and examined the lock. It was still locked. Berger raised one eyebrow in mock surprise. "As I said, someone must think we're real stupid."

"If someone did come in here we should find some evidence of dirt, or something that would indicate a person stepped in from the outside. I'll make sure the identification boys do an oblique light test in this area. And I'll have them use the electrostatic dust lifter."

With a sweep of his arm Berger indicated the two paramedics. "You talked to those two yet?"

"Nope. I'll do that now. Okay with you if I take them into the living room?"

Berger nodded and went to join the photographer videotaping the room. A still-camera swung from around his neck. "When you're done here I want a shot of the thermostat in the hallway. A good snug-up shot of the settings."

"Will do," the man responded as he continued with a detailed shot of the placement of a pillow. A

160

ruler lay on the bed to show scale. "Just about done here."

Phillip Turchyn, the Medical Examiner, stood on the far side of the bed waiting for the photographer to finish so he could make a more detailed examination of the body. A pair of latex gloves covered his hands. Berger and Turchyn had often worked together in the past, and Berger appreciated the other man's abilities.

"So, Phillip, what've we got here?"

"Officially? Suspicious death, cause unknown. Unofficially? Petechiae of the sclera and conjunctiva," he raised one of the woman's eye lids to show the small ruptures on the veins of the eyeball "Tooth imprints on the insides of her lips indicate pressure on the face, looks like it might be a suffocation. See the blue on her lips, and here, on the tips of her fingers?" He pointed to the hands on the bed but didn't touch them. "Deoxygenation led to cyanosis. And there're ruptured capillaries around the inside of the mouth."

"Any idea as to time of death?"

"That's a tricky one. Lividity would indicate four to five hours, but it's damned hot in here so that could affect my timing. Same with rigor. There's a good degree of rigor but that could be a result of the heat as well."

Berger grunted but said nothing.

"I'll bag her hands of course. If it was suffocation there's a good chance there's some hair or skin under the nails. From her position on the bed, I'd say she put up a fight. There's a bit of bruising around the shoulder area."

The photographer signalled the medical examiner to turn the body over for more photographs. Turchyn called over his shoulder to Berger, "Give me another fifteen minutes or so and I may be able to tell you more. The official report will be ready in twenty-four hours."

On his way out Berger met the identification unit. "Make sure you bag all the pillows on that bed."

Outside, on the sidewalk, he welcomed a cool breeze that stirred his thinning hair. Crime scene tape had been strung across the end of the driveway and around the property line. A group of curious neighbours and gawkers was gathered on the other side. No matter what area of the city he worked, that was one thing that never changed; the gawkers always gathered.

Hitching his pants up higher on his ample belly, he turned back to the house. A technician with a bucket of plaster was about to make a cast of one of the shoe prints in a flowerbed. It was going to be a long day, but at least there was a lot of evidence to work with.

CHAPTER EIGHTEEN

Dimitri strolled the upper corridor of Portage Place shopping centre, his footsteps echoing loudly in the nearly empty hallway. Few places on earth felt as lonely as a shopping plaza on Saturday night. With the exception of a handful of James Bond fans, there to see his latest movie, or the security guard who shuffled the bums and vagrants along, Dimitri pretty well had the place to himself. He'd spent the last half-hour passing himself off as a bored window shopper waiting for the box office to open.

Mannequins posed in stiff tableaux behind shop windows, their smiles frozen, were a poor substitute for human contact. Perhaps it was loneliness that caused his mind to play tricks on him, for a moment, one of the mannequins looked like Sonja. He shook his head to clear it and turned back towards the theatres. He had a couple of hours to kill before he paid his regular Saturday night visit to the riverbank. Even a gadgety spy movie was better than sitting in his stuffy room with its thin walls, an inadvertent eavesdropper to the drinking parties and arguments in the other rooms.

Two hours later he made his way from the theatre walking south on Kennedy Street to Broadway, then heading over to the north side of the Maryland Bridge. At the base of the bridge, behind the Miseracordia Hospital, shrubs grew untamed, forming a sheltered spot that attracted the less-favoured citizens of Winnipeg. Many were native people who preferred the unrestrained freedom of the outdoors to the Salvation Army's disciplined accommodation. Tonight the group numbered a dozen or so.

Driftwood was plentiful along the riverbank, and someone had started a small cooking fire to roast wieners. Conversation was limited, and centred on women, cheap liquor, drugs and clever tricks to make a few bucks. A slim man with the nickname of Mongoose babbled on about a fanciful scheme he was working on that would set him up for life. Few listened to his rambling fantasies.

Dimitri hunkered down on the ground a short distance from the fire but still within the fringes of the group. Here he could listen to the conversations but wasn't likely to be pressed into joining the chatter. An occasional puff of wind blew in off the river and drove the smoke, along with childhood memories of happier campfires, in his direction.

Two women poked at the fire with small sticks as they exchanged information on cooking wine. Dimitri recognized one from the Harbour Light Soup Kitchen.

"You should try at Kronos, on Sargent. That bugger doesn't care if it has to be kept behind the counter. Our money's as good as anyone else's to him."

"That stuff's just scented vinegar. I want something with a real kick."

"Well, la-de-da! I suppose you can afford cognac?"

The rattle of stones on the steep path from the street announced a new arrival. His emaciated face, sunken eyes and pockmarked arms identified him as

164

an addict with a big habit. From the light cast by the fire Dimitri could tell the man was jittery, probably in need of a fix. A thin cotton jacket was knotted securely around his waist.

"Any of you got your works with you?"

"Get lost, Walter. You wanna give us all AIDS?" The girl who spoke lounged on the other side of the fire, using a large rock as a backrest.

"Shut your trap, loudmouth! I ain't got no f-ing disease. What I got is some quality stuff and I just need""

"Get out of here, asshole!"

"You'll be sorry for that, Angel. I'm coming into some money pretty quick and""

"Yah, yah. Selling someone out to Crime Stoppers again, eh?" It was one of the men roasting wieners who spoke. Side conversations within the group ceased and all attention was directed on Walter.

"No way, man. I didn't say nothin'." Walter was visibly shaken by the accusation.

"Better watch your step, Walter. People have been killed just for associating with that group you've been hanging out with."

Several voices rose in unison to drive Walter from the fire. "Bugger off, man!"

"Yah, get the fuck outta here!"

Rebuffed, he walked a short way along the riverbank and flopped on the grass on the other side of the fire.

Careful not to appear too eager, Dimitri rose and picked his way through the shadows to Walter's side. With a sigh, he settled onto the grass and leaned back on his elbows, apparently intent on watching the action around the fire. Walter sat there, silent for a while, but his jitters soon got the best of him.

"Hey, man. You got your works with you? Maybe some grass?"

"No works, no grass, just cigarettes."

"Can you spare one, even just a half? I'm a little tapped right now, but I've got something coming in real soon."

Dimitri drew a pack of cigarettes from his jean-jacket pocket and passed two to Walter. The man smiled and tucked the spare behind his ear. He accepted a light from the match Dimitri provided.

"You're kinda new around here, eh?" Walter muttered as he drew deeply on the cigarette.

"I've been here a while. But I'm still trying to get the lay of the land, who to stay away from, what to watch out for, where to score a little walking around money. That kinda thing. You got any pointers?"

Walter spluttered a laugh that was more a wheeze. Twin jets of smoke shot from his nostrils. "I can tell ya' who to stay away from all right! Anyone in black leather who rides a hog. Give me a day or two and I'm going to haul ass out of this city." With his skinny arms crossed over his raised knees, Walter rocked back and forth to the beat of music only he could hear.

"Having a bit of a problem with the bikers, eh?" Dimitri tried to sound indifferent.

"Yah. Used to ride with a couple of them on and off. Then someone up and says I'm going to pass a tip to Crime Stoppers. What a pile of bull! Like, I've got a death wish, or what?"

"Aah. What are they worried about?" Dimitri gave a dismissive wave. "They know the cops can never nail them on anything."

"They can't nail 'em because they got no proof. But I've got the proof, man! Yes, sir, Walter's got the proof." High-pitched giggles followed his statement, then he jammed the remains of the cigarette between his lips and began snapping his fingers to his phantom song.

"Oh sure, Walter. Proof of what . . . illegal bingo parlours?"

"No man. Proof of a hit, a contract hit." The words came out in a rap song pattern, his inner music given a voice. "The bikers have contacts, back east, ya' know? There's word of a hit, a contract hit. But shh, we can't talk about it." His dirty fingers flew up to his mouth to stop the flow of words. He was so jittery his eyeballs rolled around wildly in their sockets.

The words stunned Dimitri. Was this the same contract the FBI had alerted the Mounties about? Were the bikers involved? Was someone using the bikers for a hit? If they knew about the hit it was possible they were involved, but why? Finally, his visits under the bridge might be paying off!

His mind flooded with questions he wanted to ask Walter. He had to get him away from the group under the bridge to some place where he could speak to him without arousing suspicion from the people who already mistrusted the addict.

Shouts from street level stilled all conversation. Then two police officers slid down the gravelled slope. Walter and Dimitri both rose; Walter's hands flew to the jacket around his waist.

Shit. Just what he didn't need. The way Walter was acting, they were bound to search him, and if they found anything they would haul him in for possession. Dimitri would lose his chance to get more information from a prime source. Moving slowly, he began to edge Walter further from the circle of light into the deeper shadows of the bridge footings.

"You folks realize open fires are prohibited?" One of the patrolmen walked to the centre of the group while the second circled the edge, casually working his way in the direction of Dimitri and Walter.

Walter continued to fumble with his jacket, trying to haul the incriminating evidence out of the depths of his pocket to toss it on the ground or into the river. They were almost at the pillar when Walter snagged his foot in a tangle of wire and went down heavily, his hand trapped in his pocket.

The second officer spotted the pair and sprinted in their direction. "Hey, you two! I want to talk to you." Dimitri had only a second to make his decision. If he was arrested his cover could be blown. He chose to make a run for it.

He had a good head start on the advancing patrolman and within seconds he rounded a bend. By avoiding the gravel on the river's edge he managed an almost soundless flight, and minutes later he was up the bank and onto the quiet sidewalk of Wellington Crescent.

What had happened to Walter? Had they picked him up? Chances were pretty good they would haul him in. It was also likely that with very little prodding, if he were kept away from a fix long enough, he would spill his guts about the alleged hit. Dimitri's best course of action would be to contact the cover team and let Inspector Mark Willis of CISM handle it.

He could only hope that by the time Willis waded through the bloated egos and protective layers of bureaucracy that separated the local police force and CISM, there would still be enough time to investigate, and take action, if the information proved accurate.

His brisk pace had taken him to Corydon Avenue, where he could find a phone to call Willis and catch a bus back to Main Street. Outside a coffeehouse the headlines on the late edition of the newspaper caught his eye: Wife of Prominent Businessman Dies. Under the headline was a photo of James and Rosa Sinclair.

CHAPTER NINETEEN

It was hot in the concert hall and Laury felt a tightening in the back of his neck, the foreshadowing of a headache. Tension headaches the doctor called them. Tension? Sure he was tense, but a little tension sharpened the senses, gave a person that extra edge.

Throughout the day he'd fought the urge to contact Sinclair and confirm that everything had gone as planned. Had the police found Podricki's footprints in the flowerbeds? Had Sinclair planted the physical evidence taken from the locker? The one thing he did know was that Rosa was dead, but he'd learned that from the newspapers. According to the lead article, Sinclair was questioned and released, as expected. But had he made it through the questioning without arousing suspicion?

The heavy orchestration of Mahler's Symphony No. 8 rolled through the concert hall and settled on Laury like a heavy blanket. He'd never liked Mahler's eighth, and regretted agreeing to Anel's request that they attend the performance. He could think of better ways to spend their last evening together before he left for a conference in Minnesota.

After meeting with Sinclair at Dubrovnik's, he'd realized he'd be better off if he were out of town when the evidence from Rosa's murder was submitted to the lab. He hadn't planned to attend the Minneapolis conference, but after agreeing to help

James frame Taras, he'd sent in the registration form along with the late penalty.

The official conference business would take four days, and he'd scheduled a few extra days to meet with specific equipment suppliers. By the time he got back to Winnipeg, the samples would have been examined and the results returned to the police investigators. He wouldn't be on record as having dealt with any of the evidence in the case.

"Veni, creator spiritus"

The massed voices of the huge choir called out to the creator spirit. He'd read somewhere that Mahler's inspiration for Symphony No. 8 came from his belief that the spirit could lift mankind to the highest plain of achievement. Under the circumstances, the words of the first movement haunted Laury, and a sick feeling rolled through his stomach. He ran his fingers through his hair and shifted in the seat to find a more comfortable position.

It's done now, and everything is under control. Still, from somewhere in the depths of Laury's conscience, a quiet voice whispered: Is it?

An unsettling thought slithered through his mind and refused to be banished. The janitor would be questioned. He'd be under pressure. They'd try to wear him down with their badgering. Who knew what he'd tell the investigators to get them off his back.

I should have thought it through more before I agreed to go ahead with the idea! Still, who's going to believe a suspected war criminal, especially with all the evidence they have against him?

He was worrying too much. Anyway, Taras Podricki couldn't possibly realize there was a discrepancy between the number of organs incinerated and the number kept for tests and research. The only one with access to the numbers was Anel, and that problem would be taken care of once they were married. A loving wife was less likely to snoop into her husband's business files, and if she stumbled on a discrepancy she could be convinced it was nothing more than poor bookkeeping rather than an attempt to hide anything. Everything was under control. He had covered his back.

But what if Anel said "no' to a marriage proposal. Then what? The organ market was so lucrative, it would be a shame to give it up. Well, he had a little more time now. With Rosa's murder it would be best to lie low for a while until things cooled down. He'd give Anel a month to come to a decision and then he'd move on to "plan B.'

He loosened his tie and massaged the back of his neck. The tie hadn't done the headache any good. The choir finally switched from Latin to German as they began the second movement. He really needed to get outside for some air. The concert was becoming an endurance test.

The powerful voices of the choir and the sweeping strains of the orchestra carried Anel back to the days of her childhood. Once again she was at play in the backyard as music floated through the window to surround her. Her mother was the music lover in the family. An expert pianist, she could paint pictures with a pallet of sound.

During the summer months Anel's final hour of outdoor play was usually accompanied by the music of Brahms, Beethoven, Handel or Mozart. If her mother was in a particularly light mood, there could even be some Tom Jones or Engelbert Humperdinck to finish off the session. Anel found it hard to suppress a smile as she remembered the day Marcel sang along to Am I That Easy To Forget?. He had gone all rubbery in the knees and clutched at his heart as he did a silly little parody of the singer.

Marcel. Her dragon slayer. The companion of youthful days filled with chasing kittens and fireflies and rainbows. Childhood days, when a dropped bag of popcorn constituted a tragedy. Now she was no longer a child and she could have Laury. Was he the adult equivalent of Marcel? Someone she could chase rainbows with, someone to wipe away her tears when the adult tragedies of life arrived? Or maybe she was expecting too much. Dragon slayers didn't belong in the adult world.

The thunderous applause of the appreciative audience yanked Anel from her reverie. Beside her Laury immediately rose to his feet heaving a sigh, apparently relieved it was over. Several times during the performance his fidgeting had become a distraction to Anel, and possibly to those seated around them. Now, irritation swept through her as he forced his way through the throng of people making their way down the auditorium steps to the lobby. His haste and obvious impatience bordered on rudeness.

In the lobby, Anel positioned herself well away from the congestion around the coat check while

Laury elbowed his way through the crowd to pick up her wrap.

"Well hello, Anel." The greeting came from directly behind her. It was Pamela, from the lab. "I heard a delicious rumour today. I understand congratulations are in order. Are you and our handsome director about to be engaged?"

Pamela's tone held a hint of pique, her body language belying her smile. She was a perfect example of a woman good fortune had not smiled on. It was no secret around the lab that Pamela was jealous of Anel's position of authority.

"I have no idea what you're talking about," Anel replied. "Laury and I share an interest in the symphony, nothing more." Given her present mood she found it difficult to keep her tone neutral. Where had the rumour come from? She'd made a conscious decision not to discuss her increasingly frequent outings with the lab's director with any of the staff. This type of rumour would put more pressure on her to come to a decision about her feelings for Laury.

"Then you two better get your stories straight. Laury made it quite plain in the coffee room today that he would be looking for a house in the near future. I believe he mentioned something about new wives wanting to put their signatures on their surroundings." Once again the brittle smile flickered for a moment, then faded.

The irritation Anel had managed to keep at bay all evening blossomed into smouldering anger. "Believe me, Pamela, if I have news to share about my personal life, I'll do it myself. And I would appreciate it if you wouldn't spread this story

174

around." She regretted her outburst almost immediately, but the damage was done.

All pretext of good will disappeared from Pamela's face, and it was clear to Anel that the girl had added one more reason to dislike her to an already long list.

"You know something, Anel? You're not getting any younger, careful you don't end up an old maid." Eyes flashing, she tilted her chin and stalked off to join a man who waited near the exit doors.

Laury appeared with her wrap and draped it over shoulders. Then grasping her arm, he propelled her towards the doors and the cooler night air that beckoned. The last remnants of summer light barely smudged the western sky as they made their way across Portage Avenue to the parking lot.

A police car, lights flashing, shot down Portage. Laury watched its progress, then turned to her. "Did you hear that the police suspect a biker element in the Sinclair case? If it's true, we'll probably be getting the evidence in our lab. I picked a bad time to be out of town, even if it is to Minneapolis."

"We'll be fine, I'm sure. I'll do the reports myself." The night air had calmed her. Overhead, the first of the evening stars broke through the dark sky. It was peaceful, and their steps slowed, drawing out the distance to the car. She felt Laury's touch on her arm. When she turned to him his words shattered her calm.

"Anel, I've heard Minneapolis is a wonderful place for a wedding and honeymoon."

CHAPTER TWENTY

The three men sat in the safe house, shoulders hunched and elbows on the table. Each cradled a cup of hot coffee in his hands. Tucked into a corner of the small kitchen, an ancient refrigerator wheezed its way through a cooling cycle.

Within minutes of reading of Rosa Sinclair's death, Stan had placed a call to his cover team. Rudy Savage and Ken Fairlane arrived at the house within an hour of receiving the call, having called in favours on their way over, to get as much information as possible about the death.

Although the case was still under the jurisdiction of the city police, both the police and the RCMP expected that to change. The minute organized crime activity was proven, the case would be turned over to CISC and by extension, the RCMP.

"All right. What do we know for sure?" Stan asked.

Rudy gave a quick run-down of the information he had received. "The vic was definitely Rosa Sinclair. It's too early to tell for sure, but both the evidence at the scene and the ME's preliminary report point to her having been smothered with a pillow. One of those fancy garden doors leading off the bedroom was shattered from the outside, and there were footprints around the flowerbeds and on the patio." He leaned back in his chair and scratched his receding hairline. "Crime scene boys say there were two sets of prints in the front flowerbed. One's quite a bit smaller, probably a woman's."

"Time of death?" Stan prompted.

Rudy furrowed his brow. "Hard to tell until the full autopsy report comes in. Best guess puts it sometime in the morning, anywhere between nine a.m. and noon."

The men fell silent, each lost in his own thoughts as he sorted through the information.

Ken broke the silence. "Well, now we know who the target was. Personally, I'd have put my money on Jimmy-boy rather than his old lady."

"Something's not right here, guys." Stan's fingers drummed a rhythm on the tabletop as his eyes switched back and forth between the two of them. "The timing of this is bugging me. It doesn't fit with what we know."

He stood and circled the small table as he spoke. "The FBI informs us of a hit, someone in Winnipeg, and we assume it's Sinclair. Remember, the FBI isn't tracking Canadian gangs so their information comes from somewhere in the us, probably from someone with his eye on a professional hit man. As a rule, pros don't smother, and they don't hit in the morning when people are around. I've got a contact in the Sinclair house, so I know there were at least two people at that house this morning. One of them was a gardener trimming the shrubs. Does that sound like a situation a pro waltzes into?"

"And pros don't break windows to get into people's bedrooms either," Ken added. "You're right, Stan. And if a gardener's there, that would account for one set of prints. But that leaves the

177

smaller set, maybe a woman's. Do we know of a woman with a hate-on for Sinclair's wife? One of her girls maybe?"

"Hey, wait a minute, you two!" Rudy held out his hand to stop the conversation. "Are you saying this was a hometown job? That there's a professional hit out there that hasn't happened yet?"

Stan nodded "That's exactly what I'm saying. Think about the timing here. A professional hit takes time to arrange. You don't snap your fingers and someone dies. Not with a pro. He acquaints himself with the area and the victim. He watches patterns and tries out different scenarios. This just doesn't feel like a professional job to me.

"Now, having said that, I'm going to throw a wrench into the works here." Stan quickly summarized his conversation with the junkie, Walter.

"Oh, that's just great!" Rudy groaned as he shoved his empty cup to the centre of the table. "Just what we needed. It's a professional hit, it's a biker hit. They're after Sinclair, they're after Rosa. Any other little surprises you got tucked away that you care to throw at us? Don't hold back on our account. Now's the time!"

"No surprises, just an observation. Walter definitely said it was a contract hit. How does a junkie know about a contract hit?"

"He knows about it when the contract's made with his associates," Ken answered. "In this case, his associates are the bikers. Bikers might murder other bikers to settle old scores, they don't go after . . ." His chuckle lacked mirth. "I was going to say,

178

"law abiding citizens' but I have a feeling that doesn't apply here."

"There's something else we have to consider," Rudy cut in. "Remember how one of Rosa's girls gabbed about Rosa putting pressure on James? Something about the game he had going at the lab? Maybe James felt cornered. Wouldn't be the first time a husband did the wife in when she wouldn't fall into line."

"You know, you might have something there," Stan said with a nod. "James would have had to know the bikers were getting sick and tired of Rosa pushing into their territory. If he did decide to get her out of his hair, he might have had the bikers do the dirty work for him. I've got a call in to Inspector Willis. If this investigation lands in the lap of the RCMP, he'll have no trouble having a talk with Walter. And I doubt it'll be hard to pry whatever information he has out of him." Stan poured himself another cup of coffee and leaned against the sagging kitchen counter. It was late and he suddenly felt tired.

Ken and Rudy continued to toss theories back and forth. In the end they agreed there was little to be done until they got their hands on the medical examiner's final report, and Inspector Willis sent word on his hoped-for interview with Walter.

"Hey Stan. What's the word from the contact you've got in the Sinclair house? That's the Ukrainian girl, right?" Ken asked.

At the mention of Sonja, a light tingle passed through Stan's body, a reminder that his feelings for her were not strictly professional. For the past half-hour he had been continuously pushing aside the thought that he had to call her, see if she was okay. He knew from experience what she would have gone through this afternoon; she'd have been questioned, pressed again and again for information. She would have been frightened, with no one to turn to for help or reassurance. Would they threaten to send her back to Ukraine if they didn't get the answers they wanted? Confiscate her passport? Her status here was tenuous. Rosa was her named sponsor and now Rosa was dead.

He should try to reach Sonja, both for personal and official reasons, but what would he say? Their relationship was based on a lie and now that lie would have to be exposed. He'd known all along the day would come when she would find out he wasn't Dimitri Bolenko. Now it was here. He groaned inwardly, his emotions in turmoil.

"Yah," he replied to the question. "Her name's Sonja. Trouble is, I'm not sure where she'll be right now." It's now officially a murder. The police will have sealed the house so she'll have to find somewhere else to stay. The thought weighed on Stan.

"From what you guys tell me," Stan continued, "they don't have enough on her to keep her in custody." He straightened and tried to knead some of the tension from his neck. "I'll see if I can find her and have a talk with her. Never know what information she picked up just from living in the house." His words sounded so cold.

"I've had some contact with the gardener who was there this morning, so I might get something helpful from him as well. He's the guy who was going to get me into the lab on Sunday. I might have to kiss that opportunity goodbye if the police decide to keep him. Do either of you know anyone who can fill us in on the people they've questioned?"

Rudy raised his coffee cup in response. "I've got a buddy in the Major Crimes Division. He'll have the scoop on everything that's happened. That gardener will likely be high on their suspect list. Especially if it's his footprints around the windows."

Stan was taken aback. That Taras might be involved in Rosa's murder hadn't crossed his mind. The old man certainly had reasons to dislike her, but were those reasons strong enough for murder? Over the years he'd seen people murdered for so many reasons, hate, envy, greed, jealousy, but the biggest reason was fear. Had Rosa's accusations been close enough to the truth to spark fear in the old man?

"Thanks, Rudy," Stan acknowledged with a weary smile. "We might as well wrap it up. Not much more we can do tonight anyway. Rudy, I'll phone you tomorrow for that information."

They said their goodbyes. Rudy left the apartment, followed a few minutes later by Ken. Stan rinsed out the cups to kill some time, then turned off the lights and made his way down the narrow stairs. As weary as he was, he had one more detail to take care of. He had to find Sonja.

CHAPTER TWENTY-ONE

In Taras' apartment, Sonja paced the small area between the ratty sofa and a chair, caught in the grip of a sensation bordering on hysteria. Police . . . questions . . . where were you . . . ? when did you . . . ? She couldn't even remember the answers she'd given them! It was better when the interpreter arrived and the questions were in Hungarian; at least then she could understand what they wanted to know.

Exhausted, she slumped into the shabby armchair, but was soon up re-circling the room. Rosa was dead. It was hard to imagine. Just this morning she had heard her arguing with James. She'd told the police about the argument, but they didn't seem to care. They were more interested in her shoes. They asked again and again about the gardener. They wanted to see her hands, her arms. She felt as though she were back in Ukraine! They opened her closets and drawers. They touched her things. The thought sent shivers down her spine.

She paused at the window and stared, unseeing, into the street below. It was as though a curse hung over her. Just when she thought happiness was within her grasp it was snatched away. Tears welled in her eyes. She groped for the chair and gave in to harsh sobs of despair.

The need of a tissue for her dripping nose brought her back to her senses. Crying wouldn't accomplish anything, other than releasing some tension. She felt a little better. A furry head nudged her elbow as Uncle Taras' cat, Mitska, begged for attention. She gathered the large animal into her lap and rocked back and forth, absorbing the warmth of its body as she sniffed back her tears. Mitska's contented purr brought some comfort and calmed her racing mind.

The police had questioned her, true, but they hadn't been brutal about it. One of the men had threatened to report her to the Department of Immigration because her sponsor was dead, but when he left the room another told her they wouldn't send her back if she told the truth about what had happened at the house. And in the end they had let her go. That was the important thing. They had let her go.

She gave the animal a final scratch behind the ears and set it on the floor. Exhaustion washed through her and the decrepit couch that would be her bed for the night suddenly looked very inviting. Uncle Taras had gone downstairs to the teacup reader to see if she had any extra bedding he might borrow.

With the thought of her uncle, another weight settled on Sonja's weary shoulders. He had been shocked when she arrived, almost incoherent, at his door with the news. Then she'd had to go through the story yet again. As the realization set in that he was also a suspect, he appeared to age before her eyes.

She was an added burden to him, but where else could she turn? The only other person she knew in Winnipeg was Dimitri, and she had no idea how to find him. Just getting to this apartment had been difficult.

The police had told her the Sinclair house would be cordoned off for a few days so she would have to find someplace else to stay.

"Do you know anyone in Winnipeg, Sonja?" the kind detective asked as he escorted her from the rear of the police station. "We can arrange a hotel room for you if you need one."

Tired and confused, Sonja was shocked to realize she couldn't return to the Sinclair house. Where could she go? Without thinking, she answered him, "I have an uncle . . . the gardener who was trimming the bushes today."

He looked surprised, and Sonja realized that although she had told them a gardener had been at the house, she hadn't mentioned he was her uncle. Now she had let the information slip. But what did it matter? Uncle Taras hadn't killed Rosa.

The policeman looked up Taras Podricki's address in the phone book then called for a cab. In the cab, Sonja fell into another nightmare; the driver's English was no better than hers; neither could understand the other. She finally handed him the address the policeman had written down.

It had been embarrassing to ask a man who was almost a stranger for a place to stay. Her uncle didn't even have an extra bed for her to sleep on. Tomorrow she'd have to get some toiletries from a drug store. But how much money did she have in her wallet? She was just too tired to care anymore. The chair was comfortable, and her body felt heavy. She drifted off.

Slow footsteps on the creaky stairs signalled her uncle's return and drew her back from the brink of sleep. With a great effort of will Sonja roused herself from the chair as he came in the door, his arms filled with sheets, a pillow and an extra blanket. The teacup reader had been generous with her supply of linen.

Sonja noted the grey pallor of Taras' jowly face, and realized once again the strain of his situation. How long would it be before the police found him and interrogated him as well? Police! It hit her then. She had led them right to his door when she let the officer look up the address for the cab! Sonja buried her face in her hands and fresh tears fell.

"I'm so sorry! I gave the police your name . . . so they could find your address for me. Now they know where you live. Oh, Uncle Taras! I'm so sorry!"

The old man took her gently by the shoulders and steered her towards the battered sofa. "It's not so bad as you may think, Sonja. This is Canada. The police aren't as harsh as you are used to in Ukraine. Here they ask questions and try to seek the truth. I did not kill Rosa, so what do I have to worry about?" His words were meant to calm her, but deep lines of anxiety etched his face. He made his way back to the chair she had vacated and slowly lowered himself into it.

"Yes, they will come here. Not tonight, and maybe not tomorrow, but they will come and they will ask their questions. They are very good at getting at the truth, these Canadian police." With his hands dangling between his knees, Taras bowed his head, lost deep in thought.

Sonja spread the sheets and blanket over the sofa and made what preparations she could for bed.

Finally, Taras roused himself from his contemplation. He appeared to have come to a decision and looked the better for having reached it.

"Tomorrow Sonja, when you are not so tired, we shall have a talk. There are things you will need to know. Things from the past that will affect the future."

**

From the deep shadows of a building across the street Stan watched the lighted window of the second floor apartment. Night sounds kept him company through his vigil. A cat, with a small object dangling from its mouth, triggered the light on a back alley motion sensor guarding a garage door. A man and woman passed along the sidewalk. When they saw him in the shadows, they crossed to the other side of the street. After dark, predators came in all shapes and sizes, both human and animal.

The figure of a woman crossed and re-crossed the window in the second floor apartment. For a moment she paused at the window and looked out, as though to pierce the darkness with her eyes. It was then he knew for sure it was Sonja. Instinctively, he pressed back farther into the darkness, afraid she would see him there, watching her.

He was relieved to have found her, but really, where else could she have gone? She would have seen Taras Podricki at the house today; he had promised to bring her the Ukrainian paper, and he was the only person she could turn to who understood her language.

186

No, that wasn't true. If their relationship hadn't been built on a lie, she could have turned to him. He forced the thought from his mind. He was an RCMP officer with a job to do. If she had gone anywhere other than to Taras' apartment he could have contacted her. But she did go to Taras, and he still needed Taras to get into the lab. The old man would never agree to take him through those doors if he knew Dimitri was a cop.

Fifteen minutes later the light in the apartment went out. There was nothing more he could do. Until this case was resolved he would have to stay away from her.

CHAPTER TWENTY-TWO

Anel awoke with a sharp cry, her body bathed in sweat, her throat raw. The familiar nightmare was becoming more frequent.

As usual, it began as a pleasant dream. She was in the back yard with her friend, Marcel. The sun was warm on her back, and they laughed as they played with a strange mass between them on the grass. To their delight, the object became large, then small; it bulged and shrank, continually changing shape. The game was great fun until suddenly the shape shifted once more and turned dark. She saw fear grow in Marcel's eyes as they struggled to keep the squirming mass under control. Then he came out of the garden shed, and the dark shape collapsed into a shrivelled heap.

Marcel rose to his feet. Anel knew he would leave even as she struggled to call out, to beg him to stay. Words formed in her throat, but they caught there and she choked when she strained to speak. Then Marcel was gone.

The air became thick and everything around her moved in the menacing slow motion ballet of dream-time. From somewhere in the distance she heard a low growl. Rigid with terror, she turned toward the house to call for her mother, but no sounds escaped her mouth. She felt his hand on her arm, and her throat contracted in yet another silent scream that vibrated inside her head . . .

The dream always ended the same way, with the scream.

Anel struggled to clear her mind of terror as she sat up in bed. It was just a dream. Outside rain lashed at the windows and lightening flashed, followed by the deep rumbling of thunder, the source of the growl in her dream.

Giving in to the exhaustion that clawed at her, she lay back down. Just a few more minutes, then I'll get up. Just a few more minutes . . .

When she woke again, still groggy, she was startled to see it was past noon.

Since her parents' deaths, her life had fallen into a routine. Weekdays she was able to function at work. It was the weekends that were so bad. The dreams were worse on weekends, and lately no matter how much sleep she got, it was not restful. Today she felt worse than ever. Weariness seemed to have crept into her bones, tiring her to the point of exhaustion.

The phone on the nightstand rang, helping to clear the last of the sleep from her head. It was a welcome distraction.

"Hello." Her voice sounded hoarse to her own ears and she cleared her throat.

"Anel? Are you okay?" It was Lisa. Her friend's normally bubbly voice held a note of concern.

"I'm fine. Just a bit of a sore throat I guess. No . . . actually I'm not fine. I overslept and had a terrible dream."

"Oh, Anel! You know, I'm really starting to worry about you. And that's why I'm calling. I almost get the impression you've been avoiding me lately. If I've done something to offend you I""

"No. Lisa, please. You haven't done anything wrong. It's me . . . I'm dealing with some really heavy issues."

The memory of last night came, unbidden, and she groaned silently. Should she tell her friend that Laury had proposed? That she was struggling with her answer? Pamela's taunt came back to her. ". . . not getting any younger . . . old maid."

Apparently sensing her unease, Laury had asked her to think about her answer while he was gone. That gave her a week to come to a decision. Lisa would never understand her hesitation. It was best not to mention it.

After promising to have lunch with her friend the next day, Anel ended the call. She swung her feet out of bed and forced her exhausted body to follow. Maybe if she got up and ate something she'd feel energized. But the thought of food held no appeal.

Rain, driven by sharp gusts of wind, coated the kitchen windows. Droplets tracked down the pane like tears, tears from the heavens. For whom do the heavens weep, a small voice deep inside asked. For her, of course, came the answer. Anel's own tears welled up and her throat ached with unvoiced sobs.

With a quick shake of her head she turned from the window and fought down the sorrow. She was alone too much, that was the problem. There was nothing outside of work that put any demands on her, nothing in her life that gave her any reason to look forward to events or celebrations, or even simple pleasures, like cooking a special meal. If she married Laury, she'd instantly become a member of his extended family and there would be a multitude of special occasions to give some meaning to her life.

But was that what marriage was about? Wasn't it about love, and trust, and sharing your life with someone because of who he was, not what he could give you?

Love. She desperately wanted to be loved and to love someone in return. But did she love Laury? She pushed the question from her thoughts for fear of the answer.

Trust. That was even harder. Did she trust Laury? The answer sprang into her mind with a force that shocked her. No. She didn't trust him. To trust was hard, maybe even impossible. It was easier to love, as she had loved her parents. But they betrayed her trust. So many people had betrayed her trust. Images of her dream returned and she knew it too was somehow related to betrayed trust.

There was little in the fridge to tempt her, other than some orange juice. She poured a glass and snaked a bare arm out the front door to grab the newspaper from the mailbox. The rain had sucked the summer heat from the air, leaving it cold and clammy.

The newspaper headlines and sidebars were full of the Sinclair murder. A murder in the downtown core or the north end rarely made the front pages, but when the victim was from one of the wealthy areas of town, the newspapers fell all over themselves to outdo each other. Clearly the police suspected it was gang related, so the lab would get the evidence first thing Monday morning. Work. It was something to look forward to, a distraction from her gloomy weekend.

Once more she thought of Laury. The memory of that Swiss envelope she'd found on the ground after the accident had nagged at her since that night. Why would Laury have dealings with a Swiss bank? His explanation hadn't rung true. He had lied to her, and if he'd lied to her about the envelope, what else had he lied about?

Questions crowded her mind; little things she'd pushed into the background now sprang forward clamouring for attention. If she was going to accept his proposal, she'd need to take a hard look at what was going on around her, she no longer had the luxury of allowing her life to drift aimlessly.

As she reviewed a myriad of seemingly inconsequential events with suspicion, she realized she had let a lot of things slide by unquestioned. She'd allowed Laury's explanations to go unchallenged. Why? It had been easier to accept the explanations than to become engaged in life; easier than taking an interest in something other than the day-to-day mechanics of doing her job at the lab. She really hadn't been in charge at the lab; she'd been a puppet" Laury's extension.

Anger flared for a moment, then apathy moved in to take its place. What did it matter? Laury knew what he was doing and the lab was a model of efficiency. The work was done, and done well. The staff was happy and obviously felt she was in charge. If she married Laury it might be best to quit the lab altogether and stay at home. No, that wasn't the answer either. She'd realized long ago that she was happiest with a structured routine and, she loved her work at the lab.

She sighed. It was exhausting just to think about the problem. How could she ever decide what to do?

Once more she was reminded of the image from her nightmare. Her life was like the shape that had kept shifting while she and Marcel tried to control it. It had no stability. She felt a shiver of foreboding travel through her. In her dream the shape had crumbled into a withered heap in the grass. She struggled to banish the image.

A fresh gust of wind flung heavy drops of rain against the window as she unfolded the paper and skimmed the stories that crowded the front page. Suddenly, a line of text leapt out at her ". . . owner of a successful trucking company that provides shipping services for several Winnipeg businesses, including the Central Federal Laboratory.' Her thoughts turned back to the lab and to the envelope with the Swiss stamp. If there really was a new microscope on order, it was her business to know about it. There would be records of the negotiations on file at the lab.

She was taken off guard by a hunger pang. There wasn't much to eat in the house. Reaching a decision, Anel folded the paper and rose from the table. She'd get dressed and go to the grocery store. She'd fix herself a decent meal and then, if the rain let up, she'd drive to the lab. If she was supposed to be in charge, then she should know what was going on, and she needed to know for sure if Laury had been telling her the truth about the Swiss bank.

As she tugged on a pair of jeans, a new thought came to mind. If the lab did have business dealings with Sinclair's trucking company, they were in a conflict of interest with respect to the murder evidence. It might be best to advise the police department that the samples should be shipped to the Ottawa lab for analysis. She would check the shipping records while she was there, and if Sinclair's firm was the only company they used, she'd advise the police.

CHAPTER TWENTY-THREE

Rin pounding on the poorly insulated roof drew Sonja from the depths of sleep. For a moment she was disoriented, then her eyes settled on Mitska, curled on the chair by the window, and she remembered where she was.

Uncle Taras' voice greeted her from the tiny kitchen area.

"Good morning, Sonja. I'm fixing coffee. Do you take it black, or with milk and sugar?"

"Black, thanks." As she sat up she realized she'd slept in her clothes, and then the horrible events of yesterday flooded her memory. The police hadn't even allowed her to take a change of clothes from the house.

Freshly brewed coffee scented the air and drew her to the table. Her uncle had obviously made an early morning trip to the grocery store, for half a grapefruit sat on a chipped plate and an empty bowl flanked a box of unopened breakfast cereal. When she turned to smile her thanks, he shrugged shyly and drew his hands through his thinning hair. He looked tired, as though he hadn't slept well.

"I hope it's okay. Breakfast . . ." He shrugged. "I usually just have coffee."

While she ate they spoke of the rain, Miranda's phoney teacup readings, anything other than the news that surely dominated the front-page headlines in the newspaper that lay folded by the sink. Finally, as the coffee pot yielded its last drop, Taras cleared his throat, a sign that now they would speak of the important things he had alluded to the previous night.

"We are both caught in circumstances over which we have no control. I had nothing to do with Mrs. Sinclair's death, but of course I am a suspect. We quarrelled in the past, she made accusations . . ." His hands scribed vague circles in the air. "I have much in my past to be ashamed of, Sonja, and these things may become known because of the police investigation. Even though the police will find nothing to charge me with, perhaps it is time my secrets are taken from their hiding place and brought into the light."

"Uncle Taras, maybe your secrets should be left where they are. Whatever happened was so long ago. What can be accomplished by speaking of them now? This is a new country and a new time. You don't have to bring the old business with you."

"There you are wrong, Sonja. I have brought the old business with me. There are some things in one's past that you bring with you whether you like it or not. I have brought my shame with me."

Using the table for support, he rose from his chair and went to a set of drawers beneath the kitchen counter. The drawer he chose was sticky, reluctant to open, and it was an effort for him to tug it free. He drew a package from its depths and made his way back to the table.

"Here is my shame, Sonja. This is why your father refused to allow my name to be spoken in your family. Somehow he found out, or perhaps he only sensed what I had done. When he confronted me, I refused to answer the accusations. He read the guilt in my face, and told me never to show myself

196

at his door again or he would report me to the authorities."

The package sat on the table between them. Its wrapping was old and only loosely attached with a slack rubber band. Obviously, it had been opened and closed many times over the years. Sonja lifted her eyes from the bundle on the table, her question obvious, needing no voice.

"If you open the package you will see two chocolate covered eggs. But to know what is really in the package you must return with me to the days of the Second World War.

"As I told you the other day, I was the orderly for Obersturmfuhrer Widenmayer. He was an evil man, totally without a sense of morality. He had power and felt free to use it for his own gain. When we entered Russia, all was in chaos. Peasants and ordinary citizens in the path of the German army fled as best they could. But there were others, those in positions of authority, or who had something to bargain with, who did not have to take their chances with the common people.

"Obersturmfuhrer Widenmayer had confiscated the apartment of a senior official in one of the district centres. The official did not flee, but went into hiding. Shortly after we arrived, he sent a message to Widenmayer saying that he had something he wished to discuss with the Oberstrumfuhrer. The note said he was sure Widenmayer would find the time well spent. I remember the way he smiled when he received the note" this was not the first time he had been contacted with requests for meetings. The Obersturmfuhrer had sent several packages back to

Germany with treasures he'd either seized or received as gifts."

He paused for a moment, his eyes fixed on the box with the eggs, and then continued. "On the evening of the meeting Widenmayer arrived home late and I was in the kitchen, preparing a tray with a light meal. There was a knock on the door and Widenmayer answered it himself. I overheard the discussion between the two men.

"The official said he had two Faberge eggs in his possession and would be willing to give them to Obersturmfuhrer Widenmayer in exchange for safe passage for himself and his family.

"Bah! Where would you get Faberge eggs? What do you take me for? A fool!' Widenmayer said to the man.

""No, Herr Widenmayer. Not a fool. I will explain. After the fall of the Czars the eggs became the property of the Soviet people. Insured by Lloyds of London, they were put on display so the people could see the wealth the Czars had obtained off the backs of ordinary people. Some of the eggs were sent on a tour to raise money for the country. When war broke out the eggs were here, in the City museum, on display. Of course, they were immediately removed from display for safekeeping, but now perhaps they could become lost. Records have a way of disappearing during times of war. And who will search too diligently for them when they are insured by such a huge insurance company?'

"Within a few days a package was delivered to the apartment. I was sure it was the Faberge eggs."

Taras unwrapped the bundle and smoothed out the paper, but did not open the battered box.

"The Obersturmfuhrer didn't send this package home. Perhaps he felt the contents were too precious to trust to couriers, or perhaps he wanted the eggs near him so that he could admire their beauty. I never actually saw the eggs until many months later.

"The fortunes of the war had shifted in favour of the Soviets and their American allies. We were driven back and were under constant attack. One day the building we were living in suffered a direct hit, and the Obersturmfuhrer was killed. I rushed to his room, but there was nothing I could do for him. He wasn't a kind man and I did not waste any tears on him."

Taras fell silent for a moment, as though reliving the desperate last days of the falling empire. Once more he cleared his throat, then continued: "I went through his things to gather his personal papers so they could be sent to his family. I found the package containing the eggs in his footlocker." His eyes rose to meet those of his niece and she saw the torment there. "I didn't include the eggs in the package, Sonja. They didn't belong to Herr Widenmayer; they belonged to the Russian people. At first I told myself I would make sure they got back to the people . . . but I was deluding myself. I was no better than the man I despised. Like Herr Widenmayer, I took them from their package at night and looked at them. They were so beautiful!

"At the end of the war I brought the eggs home, but what could I do with them? All of Europe was on the lookout for stolen art treasures. They bewitched me, these eggs of the Czars!"

Stunned by the revelation, Sonja opened the lid of the stout box and drew out what appeared to be a chocolate egg. It was large, the size of a goose egg, and quite heavy. The chocolate was old and grainy; in some places it had been damaged and then either heated to reseal it, or moistened and smeared to heal the break. "You dipped them in chocolate?" she asked, her voice barely audible.

"Yes. When I decided to leave Ukraine I could not leave them behind. I heated chocolate and dipped them, again and again, until they were coated in a deep layer. When I went across borders, the inspectors saw only chocolate eggs. If they asked, I told them they were presents for my nieces in Canada."

Sonja drew the second egg out of the box and laid it beside the first on the table.

"They have brought only misfortune to those who have possessed them, Sonja. Since the day I touched them I have been a haunted man. They must go back to the Russian people, and I ask that you return them."

"Me? You want me to return them? I don't understand."

"I am an old man, my child. I know that I do not have much time left. And now, with this business . . . the police . . ." He sighed and drew his hands over his face then rose, and with shuffling steps made his way to the window where he peered out at the falling rain. "Remember when I said that the eggs were insured by Lloyds of London? After the war they paid out the insurance money but posted a reward for the return of the eggs. If something happens to me, I want you to return them. The reward will be paid to you for returning war treasures, no questions asked."

"Oh, no! No, Uncle Taras""

Her objection was cut short by the sound of two sets of footsteps climbing the creaky stairs to the second floor.

Turning back to the window, Taras peered into the street below where a police cruiser was parked at the curb. "Ah, I see the waiting game is over." He quickly scooped the eggs back into the box, wrapped the paper around it and stretched the rubber band to hold the mess together. The band snapped and hung limply in his hands. For a moment he hesitated, then shoved the bundle into the drawer, forcing it shut.

A heavy knock sounded on the door. Sonja's eyes flew from the drawer to her uncle's drawn face, then back to the door where the knocking continued.

"Yes, yes. Do not be so impatient. I am coming," he called as he made his way to the door and the police waiting on the other side.

*＊＊

Taras balled his fist and brought it down on the marred top of the table in the interrogation room. "I tell you for the final time, I was there at the house cutting the shrubberies. Yes, I cut the shrubbery beside the patio door of Mrs. Sinclair's bedroom, but I did not look in. And yes, the ground was wet from the sprinklers. Mr. Sinclair said the sprinklers had not been working properly that morning. Now, if you want to charge me with something please do so. If not, I have to go home so I can get ready for

201

work. I work at the lab, and it has to be cleaned for Monday morning."

Detective Sergeant Michael Berger watched the old man rise to his feet. Berger didn't protest. They had been questioning him for hours and his story hadn't changed. Anyway, he knew in his gut that Taras Podricki hadn't smothered Rosa Sinclair.

Rosa was a big woman and she would have been fighting for her life. This man would have had the strength thirty years ago, but now he was too frail. A tinge of grey lightened the area around Podricki's lips and several times during the interrogation Berger had noticed him drawing air through his mouth, as though he was short of breath.

"We'll have a squad car drop you off if you'd like." At first Berger thought Podricki would protest, but after a moment he nodded in assent. "And would you be willing to leave us a hair sample, Mr. Podricki?"

Anger flared in the older man's eyes. Then with a swift movement he ran a hand through his thin hair, gave a yank, and deposited the result on the table. Squaring his shoulders, he turned and stalked from the room.

Berger lost the battle to keep the grin from his face. There was still a lot of piss and vinegar in the old bastard. He would hate like hell to find the hair matched the sample they'd found clasped in one of Rosa's hands.

CHAPTER TWENTY-FOUR

By the time Dimitri arrived at the lab, the chilly late summer rain had stopped, but the sky still churned with low, dirty-grey clouds. Greasy puddles of water flared briefly with light as the occasional vehicle passed on the street, headlights probing the post-storm gloom.

Would the old man show? A contact within the police department had told him Taras had spent several hours in interrogation, but had been released with plenty of time to make it home, eat supper, and get ready for work.

At ten minutes to seven Taras turned the corner from the direction of William Street and approached the double front doors of the building. It was obvious the day had taken a toll on the older man, his shoulders drooped, his steps were slow. The brown bag in his left hand hung limply at his side.

"Greetings, vuiko. Did you remember we had an appointment tonight?" Dimitri tried his best to sound upbeat, unaware of the recent events.

"Yes, yes. I remembered," the older man muttered. "And call me Taras. Today I have no wish to be reminded of the old country." Dimitri tugged one of the heavy glass doors open and motioned Taras into the building ahead of him.

A security guard seated at a desk in the large limestone and glass foyer raised his hand in greeting when he recognized the older man. As the door sighed shut behind them Taras paused, placing his hand on Dimitri's arm.

"Do you read the papers, my young friend?"

"No, not often. The English, you know . . ." Dimitri answered.

"Well, you might like to know that your friend, Sonja, has had to come and stay with me. Her employer was murdered yesterday. Unfortunately, I was also at the house trimming the hedges, so I have had to give an accounting of my movements to the police." He sighed heavily and continued toward the desk.

Dimitri was glad of the reprieve, as it gave him time to think of a response. Taras greeted the guard and explained Dimitri's presence in the lab. They chatted about fishing for a minute as Taras signed them in. The guard handed them the entrance badges, then Taras and Dimitri turned toward the second security door. Taras passed his card across the optical viewer to gain entry.

Feigning shock, Dimitri took up the conversation. "The Sinclair woman was murdered? Was Sonja there? Is she okay? What luck for her that I introduced the two of you the other day, at least she had someplace she could go."

"She was on an errand when Mr. Sinclair found the body, but they did question her. She is shaken, but she'll be all right. And yes, it's a good thing she was able to find me." They negotiated the ramp and hallways to the entrance of P-Block, the mechanical operations unit, where Taras would have to swipe his pass card. He stopped for a moment and looked Dimitri in the eye as he spoke. "There's more to her coming to my apartment than a need for a place to stay. I'm that uncle she was looking for."

This time Dimitri's shock was not an act. "What the...! The picture. In the album. You saw a resemblance in the old black and white picture." The words were out before he could stop them. Damn! That's what comes from getting too close to someone in a case, you lose your edge.

Suspicion crept into Taras' face. "You're quite observant, my young friend. Why is that?" Dimitri scrambled for an answer. I've blown it. He may be old but he's still sharp. "You need to keep your wits about you when you live in the Ukraine these days. I've learned to watch and listen, and to keep my mouth shut. Now, I'm curious to see these wonderful sterilizers of yours. Let's have a look." Dimitri started down the corridor, but Taras didn't follow immediately.

Dimitri's explanation had sounded lame, even to his own ears. He had aroused the old man's suspicions at the worst possible time. When he glanced over his shoulder, he saw Taras still in the middle of the corridor, an intense look of concentration on his face. Dimitri stopped and waited for him to catch up and lead the way down the corridor to the viewing chamber of the sterilization room. As the older man passed, Dimitri noticed a slight sheen of perspiration on his temples. Was the old man getting ill?

"So! Here we are," Taras said with pride as he gestured to the large solid waste sterilizer, and the wastewater purification tank beside it. "Look at that. Is there anything similar in the entire USSR?"

Dimitri heaved a silent sigh of relief. Taras seemed to have let his suspicions die. "There is no

USSR anymore, old man. Ukraine is now a free country."

"Bah! Does that mean there is a change? It's still the same people in charge as before."

"Let's not get into politics, please. I left Ukraine behind. Tell me about this fabulous sterilizer of yours. How does it work?"

Taras was quickly caught up in discussing the mechanics of the sterilizer. Dimitri listened to the explanation with mild interest, then asked, "How do they register the specimens that are disposed of?"

"There is a log book for that. The shipment is recorded in the unit upstairs by a number, and is marked as either an organ or some other specimen. When I remove it from the unit, I sign the book. Down here, the tissue is put in the sterilizer and heated to a hundred and twenty-one degrees for an hour. It's also pressure treated in the tank. In a sense, it's rendered. There's not a bacteria, virus or fungus that can survive the treatment. That they guarantee."

"Aren't you afraid you're going to catch some disease when you handle the tissue?"

"Oh, no! I don't handle the organs or tissue. They're sealed in thick protective wrap and I wear gloves when I transport it. Of course I wouldn't handle diseased flesh without protection!" He waved a dismissive hand in the air.

"Does anyone ever check to see if the records are correct? That everything in the book has been removed and sterilized?"

The older man shrugged, then peered keenly at Dimitri. His eyebrows slowly rose to meet his receding hairline. "Sometimes Dr. O'Connor checks the procedure. Other times he's asked for my transportation log. But why the interest in that?"

Damn! The suspicion wasn't dead. The man was still wary. "Just curious I guess. Come on, I'll give you a hand with the cleaning. I want to see this marvellous laboratory unit of yours." He'd have to leave well enough alone. The old man was on guard now. Short of actually helping with the removal and examining a package labelled as an "organ,' there was nothing more he could learn here.

On the walk back to the unit, Dimitri speculated about the potential for making money for anyone who had access to organs, and the guts to tamper with the records of the sterilization procedure. When "research organs' came into the lab did they leave via the sterilizer? Or did they leave for the airport within minutes of arriving via the Sinclair trucking company?

***

Anel watched the sun set through her kitchen window. Clouds backlit by the fading light appeared bruised, pounded and beaten by the wind and rain. She decided to follow through on her decision to go to the lab. It felt good to take some control of her life, even if it was to check up on her possible future husband. She tossed together a quick omelette for supper, then pulled on a thick green sweater to ward off the damp chill of the evening, and left her apartment. Sunday evening traffic was light and twenty minutes later she pulled into the parking lot.

"I'll have to get you to sign in, miss," the night guard stated as Anel entered the doors of the two-story foyer. He thumbed the volume down on his portable radio, swung the black binder around on the counter and handed her a pen. "Not a nice night to have to come in to work. Looks like summer's headin' out of town."

Anel smiled an acknowledgement and added her name to the line under Taras Podricki's signature. She'd met the janitor on a few other occasions when she'd worked late. He seemed like a nice enough guy who did his job well and kept to himself. "I'll probably be less than an hour," she told the guard as she made her way through the second set of glass doors.

She didn't have to go through with it, she reminded herself as she used the stairs to the second floor. She could just check the shipping records, and if the company was indeed Sinclair's trucking company, she could leave it at that and go home. In the morning she could call the major crimes division and have them send the Sinclair murder evidence to the lab in Ottawa and that would be the end of it. She didn't have to check the purchasing records for a major equipment purchase. She didn't have to check up on Laury's story about the Swiss Bank envelope.

At the far end of the unit, near the row of offices, a light was on, and she could see Taras leaning over his cleaning cart. Movement a few offices farther along the row caught her eye. Someone was cleaning in Laury's office. That was odd. She was sure Taras was the only cleaner authorized on this floor. Anel didn't bother to flip on the bright overhead lights as she moved along the rows of benches and machines towards the two figures at the far end of the floor.

"Mr. Podricki," she called as she moved closer to the light. "What's going on here?"

Taras gasped and turned toward her. He was in obvious distress. His face was coated with perspiration; his mouth set in a grim line of pain. From the corner of her eye she saw the second man approach from her left, but before she could turn to confront him, Taras grunted and collapsed against the cart.

"Taras!" the man shouted as he rushed to assist the stricken cleaner. Anel moved quickly to help lower Taras to a sitting position on the floor, then she turned to confront the stranger.

From the condition of his clothes she guessed he was a working man down on his luck. He reached out to place his hand on her arm but she drew back quickly. "What are you doing in this building? How did you get in?"

"Miss, this man needs an ambulance. Can you show me where the nearest phone is?" Did she see a plea in his eyes now? He laid his hand along the side of Taras' face, running his thumb along the old man's cheekbone. There was gentleness in the caress.

Still numb with shock at the sight of an unauthorized stranger in the secure building, Anel rose to her feet. "I'm sorry, but I'll have to call"" Her words were cut off by another groan from Taras.

The stranger ignored her words and turned his attention back to the stricken man. He loosened the buttons of the cleaner's shirt, then supported Taras in his arms, as though he were a child. "Hold on, Taras. We're calling an ambulance."

Although struggling for breath, Taras forced out the words. "I know you are not who you say you are. I am an old, sick man, but I still have my wits about me. What do you want with me? Who are you?"

Even Taras didn't know who the man was! Anel's concern was quickly replaced by panic. She had to call the police.

"Call an ambulance," the man shouted at her over his shoulder. "Please! Call right now!"

She stepped over to the nearest desk and dialled 911, but her eyes never left the man kneeling on the floor beside the cleaner. It was obvious that he meant no harm to Taras. In fact, he seemed frantic to get help. She would ask the 911 operator for both the police and an ambulance.

As though reading her mind, the intruder spoke. "I'm an undercover RCMP officer investigating this lab. Don't ask for the police." He held her gaze for a moment, then turned back to Taras.

"Taras, did you hear me? I'm an RCMP officer. I'm investigating the lab and James Sinclair. I mean neither you nor Sonja any harm, that I promise you. An ambulance is on the way, but I'm going to have to leave you. I'll tell Sonja what's happened and help her get to the hospital."

Taras' reply was very weak, and Anel struggled to hear the words over the ringing of the phone in her ear. "Help Sonja . . . eggs must go back . . . the money . . ." Then he lost consciousness.

The 911 operator was on the line. Anel quickly explained the situation and hung up. Before she could confront him for answers, the man was at her side.

210

"I need your help. I need you to trust me."

CHAPTER TWENTY-FIVE

"Hold on, Taras. An ambulance is on its way." Anel gave his hand a squeeze to reassure him of her presence. His eyes were closed, his hand limp in hers. Did he even know she was there?

Several long minutes crept by, then finally a sharp ping announced the arrival of the elevator. The doors opened to reveal a tight knot of people. Two para-medics rolled out a gurney. The security guard from downstairs found the main light panel and with a flip of the switch, the entire room sprang into stark relief under a harsh fluorescent glare. Anel's anxiety deepened when she saw two men dressed in blue uniforms follow the para-medics down the main aisle of the room. They were policemen.

"If you move aside, Miss, we'll take it from here." Her nod was mechanical. She got up from the floor where she'd been kneeling beside Taras, and stepped back. With practiced efficiency, the para-medics moved the limp man to the gurney and slipped an oxygen mask over his ashen face.

One of the policemen approached her and flipped open a small notebook. His manner was matter-of-fact, a sharp contrast to the tension among the others gathered around the prostrate figure on the gurney. "We'd like to ask you a few questions. Can I have your name, please?"

The mysterious stranger was right. He thought the police might respond since the 911 call had come from the lab. For a moment she wavered.

Common sense told her she should tell the police what had really happened, and let them deal with it. Then she remembered the gentleness of his touch on Taras' cheek. Woman's instinct overrode common sense and confirmed her decision not to mention the man who claimed to be an undercover agent. Swallowing hard, she tried to control the shaking of her hands as she answered the questions.

Satisfied with her straightforward answers, the police officer flipped his notebook shut and returned it to his breast pocket.

Within minutes of arriving on the floor, the gurney carrying Taras made the return trip to the elevator where the security guard waited with his override key. "Where will you take him?" Anel asked as they manoeuvred the bed into the cramped space.

"Health Sciences Centre. It's just a few blocks away. He's one lucky man that you decided to come in to work tonight."

Anel nodded, then hugged herself as if to ward off a chill. Too much was happening too fast. Would the security guard remember the stranger Taras signed in when they entered the building? Or was he too upset with his friend's condition to think beyond what was happening here and now? The guard followed the gurney into the crowded elevator without speaking to the police officers.

One of the officers gave the cleaning cart a quick examination but found nothing out of the ordinary. When he re-joined them, the team bid Anel good night and made its way slowly across the large room, stopping occasionally to peer with interest at the assorted machinery and diagnostic equipment.

"We may as well take the stairs. I know you could use the exercise," one joked as he pushed open the door to the stairwell.

"Hey! Careful. Has my wife been crabbin' to you about my weight?" came the reply. A burst of male laughter echoed up the stairwell as the fire door hissed shut behind them.

Exhaling, Anel slumped into the nearest chair with her head in her hands. The overhead lights flickered off, and a few seconds later a hand descended to rest lightly on her shoulder.

"Thanks," the intruder said.

She twisted out of the chair and away from his hand. "Don't be too quick to say "thanks.' If you don't give me a decent explanation of what's going on here, I'll be very quick to call the police back." Light spilling from the office next to them revealed the tension on his face.

"You deserve an explanation, and you'll get one. But before I start, how much I tell you hinges on your answer to just one question." He motioned to the abandoned chair, an invitation for her to sit, but in a show of defiance, she crossed her arms and began to pace the area between two work benches.

"No! Before we start, I want to know who you are."

He nodded. "That's fair. First of all, despite my scruffy appearance, I am an RCMP officer. My name is Stan Bolenko. I'm working undercover on a case that's become something of a maze. One trail led to another which eventually led me here, to the lab."

"How do I confirm that what you're telling me is the truth?" She had been stupid. She should have told the police someone else was in the unit, someone without authority to be there.

Despite the harsh tone of her words, he smiled. "I can give you a phone number Ms . . ."

The question hung there. She was forced to answer. "Blondeau. Anel Blondeau."

"I'd be happy to give you a phone number where you can confirm my identity."

His polite manner and apparent sincerity were disarming. Suddenly, Anel felt foolish. Still, women's intuition only went so far, she would check on his story. A few minutes later she hung up the phone. The officer on the other end had confirmed that Stan Boyko was indeed an undercover RCMP officer.

Stan perched on the edge of a desk and took a deep breath. "Okay. What's your connection with this lab?"

Anel's apprehension gave way to a deep sense of foreboding. He had told Taras he was investigating the lab and James Sinclair. That meant the RCMP suspected the lab of illegal activity! "I work here . . . I'm the supervisor of the analysis department."

He studied the battered toe of his running shoe for a moment, then brought his gaze up to meet hers. "As I mentioned, our investigation into illegal activity has led us to an individual at this lab."

"And you used Taras Podricki to get in here?" It was difficult to keep the condemnation from her voice.

He seemed uncomfortable. "The trail led here. Taras worked for an individual named James Sinclair, and James Sinclair has ties to the director of this lab, Laury O'Connor. Sinclair managed to get Taras a""

For a moment the room skidded out of focus as her head spun with his words. "Anel?" His voice seemed to come from a distance. The sharp taste of bile burned in the back of her throat. She felt his hand on the back of her neck, then her head was forced between her knees. The spinning stopped, and the room aligned itself once more.

With one hand she drew the hair back from her face while she held tightly to the arm of the chair with the other. "Are you telling me that you suspect that the director of this lab is involved in criminal activity?"

"Yes. Well . . . actually, at this point it's only a suspicion. But we're following some solid leads. You work here, Anel. You know what happens on a day-to-day basis. Can you help me check the records for organs that come in from the hospitals? They're probably marked as research organs."

"We get a lot of research organs! Dr. O'Connor is doing work on organ rejection. He can't do his research without them. There's nothing illegal about that."

"I understand. But, if what I suspect is true, some of these organs aren't used for research at all. If I can get into the shipping records, I'll be able to check whether or not priority shipments were sent to the airport on one of Sinclair's trucks the same day research organs were delivered here to the lab."

"You suspect he's re-selling these organs?"

Stan nodded. "There's a huge black market for organs in Europe. Of course, the second scenario may be that he's reselling research quality organs. He could fake tests, and then mark them as having been disposed of. If I'm right, the organs are sold through the Ukrainian mafia and O'Connor and Sinclair are paid via accounts in Switzerland."

She was aware of his voice, but no longer huddled in the chair of the semi-darkened lab. She was picking up an envelope with a Swiss stamp on it. She was signing for a cooler delivered from a teaching hospital. She was making a list of research organs and tissue to be sterilized, material she had never actually seen. Laury had given her a hand written list to re-do on the disposal form. How many deliveries had she accepted, or prepared for shipment, that she really knew nothing about? She had been given instructions and had followed them, never questioning, never becoming fully involved in what should have been her job.

"You have no idea what you're asking me to do." The words were difficult to force through numb lips. "I'm the one who prepares the disposal forms."

Stan squatted on the floor and gripped her limp hands in his. "Anel, I really need your help. Have you ever noticed a discrepancy between the forms and the log book? Do you have access to the delivery records?"

She nodded and, disengaging her hands from his, rose from the chair. This was just like her dream, "had it been an omen? Her world was crumbling. She had come here tonight to check the delivery records. So she would do that. If the

217

majority of the deliveries were with Sinclair Trucking Company then she would check one organ delivery date" just one. If that matched a shipment date . . . It was hard to think beyond that. She retrieved the key to the filing cabinet and led the way to the records room.

Within minutes it was obvious something was terribly wrong. Time after time the dates of deliveries from teaching hospitals matched deliveries to the airport with Sinclair Trucking Company. It would be more difficult to determine if there were discrepancies between the log book and the tissue disposal forms. She would know more if she could speak with Taras Podricki about it. But what if Taras was involved too?

"Do you think Taras has something to do with falsifying the sterilization records?" Anel flipped the switch to turn on the photocopier in a corner of the file room.

"No," Stan replied. He laid another requisition slip aside to photocopy. "I think this business is tied in with Rosa Sinclair's death, and I think Taras is being framed for her murder. Maybe I'd better fill you in on what's happening here." He set aside the pile of paper and turned his attention to Anel.

"We're pretty sure Sinclair and O'Connor are involved in the Ukrainian mafia. With Rosa's death, the mafia is sure to be nervous about their operations here in Winnipeg. Taras was one of the few who could raise an alarm about what's going on in this lab. The way I see it, framing him for her murder would eliminate a threat to the lab and draw suspicion away from her real killer. If Taras is being framed, then it's a good indication that Sinclair, and the organization he's involved with, were behind her murder."

Anel set aside her sense of foreboding. She needed to clear her head, think rationally. "You think our janitor is being framed for Rosa Sinclair's murder? How . . . how is that possible?"

Stan explained how Taras had gone to the house to trim the bushes and left his footprints around the patio door. "According to the police, Rosa grabbed a handful of hair from her assailant. Taras told me they asked him for a hair sample today. He was pretty shook up about it. Said he was so mad that he pulled some hair out, slammed it on the table in the interrogation room and walked out.

"When you think about it, it's not surprising he had this heart attack. The past couple days have been pretty stressful on the old guy." Stan shook his head.

With shaky hands Anel took the requisition forms to the copier, stacked them in the feeder and hit the start button.

"Even if it is Taras' hair they've found, I'd be willing to put money on it that it's been planted there. You're the analysis specialist, Anel. Can a lab tech tell if hair has been pulled out at the scene?"

Her eyebrows drawn down in a frown, Anel gave her attention to the question. After a few moments of thought she nodded.

"There's a good possibility a tech could spot the difference. Hair that's been planted would probably come from a comb, or it may have been picked off a sweater. That hair would have been shed naturally, so there wouldn't be a root attached to it. Hair that's pulled out would have a root, perhaps even a skin tag. If the hairs at the scene"" She stopped in mid-sentence as a memory hit her with an almost physical force. The locker check!

Stan cocked his head, but said nothing, allowing her to collect her thoughts. Although she tried to keep calm, as the incriminating evidence mounted, her control was slipping. As she told him about the sweep for antibiotic resistant strains of bacteria, her voice was so shaky she had difficulty forming her words.

"I know for a fact that he checked Taras' locker. If what you're saying is true, then he could have taken the hairs from the locker." She stopped and tears filled her eyes. "I've helped him do these things. I'm part of it, too."

For Stan, the knowledge that Laury O'Connor had gained access to Taras' locker was one more piece of evidence that pointed to his involvement in both the organ trafficking and Rosa's death. His sympathy for Anel rose as he saw the effect of this new revelation on her. She seemed to be a vulnerable young woman, easy prey for a manipulator.

"Anel, this would be a good time for you to tell me what you know about the organ procedure."

In a monotone, she recounted the process for accepting organs, how they were catalogued and how the sterilization logs were filled in to document the disposal process.

"But there's more. I should probably tell you about something that happened just a few days ago." She recounted finding the letter with the Swiss stamp and her doubts about Laury's explanation. "If he was negotiating with the bank

220

I'm sure we can find the contract in the records." She turned and started toward a bank of cabinets near the window but mid-way she stopped as harsh sobs racked her body.

Something else was going on here that Stan didn't understand. The woman was falling apart in front of his eyes. He caught her and held her in his arms.

"Laury . . . Dr. O'Connor and I have become quite close these last few months." She fought to keep her growing hysteria down, but her voice raised a notch as she continued. "He's asked me to marry him."

That explained it! Her world was falling apart before her eyes. When the storm faded, he eased her into a chair. How could he leave her like this? But he had to get the copied way-bills to Inspector Willis. They'd want to move on O'Connor before he got wind of the turn of events. "I think we're finished here. I'm going to take these photocopies with me and turn them over to someone who can take over the investigation from his end. Are you going to be okay?"

She turned her tear-stained face to him and wiped at the wetness with the back of her hand.

"I'll phone someone who can take you home if you'd like. And I'll need Laury O'Connor's home address."

"He's not here," she managed around the occasional dry sob that still shook her. "I mean . . . he's gone to a conference in Minneapolis. Please, don't leave me alone right now."

Since O'Connor was out of town, Stan didn't need to move quite as fast as he'd first thought. His first priority could be getting hold of Sonja; she needed to know about her uncle. Realizing he could use a woman around when he broke the news, he nodded and gathered up the photocopies. "Come on, there's someone I want you to meet, then we'll check on Taras."

They made the trip to Taras' building in Anel's car, riding in silence, each deep in thought.

Sonja's smile of greeting when she opened the door of the apartment faded to an expression of curiosity when she saw Anel.

"Sonja," Stan said in Ukrainian. "I have some very bad news for you." He took her hands in his and looked her in the eye as he spoke. "Your uncle became sick at the lab. He's been taken to the hospital."

She snatched one hand free to cover her mouth and her gaze flew from Stan to Anel, then back again. "No!" she whispered into her hand. "Please, tell me this is not true."

His heart ached for her. What was worse, he would have to tell her so much more that would hurt her before the night was over.

He turned to indicate Anel and spoke in English. "This is Anel, a friend of your uncle's, from the lab. Come on, we're going to take you to the hospital."

Sonja grabbed her sweater from the back of a chair and tugged it on as they left the apartment.

At the hospital their worst fears were confirmed. Taras Podricki had not survived the trip. He had died in the ambulance.

CHAPTER TWENTY-SIX

Monday Morning

"You're sweating like a bloody pig. Have a seat, and calm down." Dennis Foster felt little sympathy for the man pacing back and forth in front of his desk.

"What? Now I should control how much I sweat? Sit down! Stand up! Do this! Do that! What am I? Some damned marionette who dances when you pull the strings?" James Sinclair wiggled his shoulders in a parody of a dance, and then continued his diatribe. "James, your wife is getting too nosy. You're going to have . . ."

Foster shot out his hand to stop the flow of words. "Hold it right there! I don't want to hear any more."

James braced himself on the wide desk, leaned across it, and stabbed a trembling finger at the lawyer. "No! You hold it right there, counsellor. Don't give me any of that crap about not wanting to hear a confession. You and I both know you'll defend me whether you want to or not. You're no better off than I am, when you think about it. Just how often do they pull your strings? Hmm?"

As James drew back from the desk, a sweaty palm print marred the shine of the mahogany surface.

Foster eyed the glistening spot with disgust. The disgust slowly turned to horror as the implications of the moist print sunk in: James was probably a secreter, someone who shed an abundance of DNA markers in body fluids. With a few long strides, Foster covered the distance to the wet bar and splashed amber liquid into two glasses. The city was just crawling out of bed and he was already into the sauce. His wife was right, he had a drinking problem.

James joined him at the bar and accepted one of the glasses before he moved to contemplate the view of the city seventeen stories below the window.

"Let's talk a little bit about this sweating problem you have." Foster nodded in the direction of leather chairs grouped around a low table in the centre of the room. From long experience, he knew that a difficult client tended to cooperate a little better when ensconced in the buttery folds of one of the chairs, than when facing him across his imposing desk.

Turning from the window, James rocked back and forth on his heels. "It's genetic. My father was the same way. A little excitement and he dripped buckets. What is this? You want to be my doctor now, as well as my lawyer?" Once Foster was seated, James followed suit.

"I'm assuming that on the morning of Rosa's murder you would be experiencing a little excitement yourself? So . . . say if you happened to grip a pillow, there would be a good chance some sweat was left on that pillow?"

The import of the question wasn't lost on James. He took a minute before he answered. "Yeah, there'd be sweat on it. And our maid can honestly say Rosa and I hadn't slept in the same room for years. But, there was some hair found at the scene that wasn't mine, and what about the footprints outside the window?"

"We're not dealing with the Keystone Cops here, James. Muddy footprints outside, but none in the room?" A pause carried the depth of his scorn. "Anyway, that discussion is moot. The old man died this morning of a heart attack. And, to complicate things further, I received word this morning that the crime scene evidence is being sent to the Ottawa lab because of rumours that the lab here is compromised." Foster watched, fascinated, as the colour fled from Sinclair's face.

"This isn't the way it was supposed to play out," James muttered. "What are my options? A plea bargain?"

"Have you thought this through?" Foster found it difficult to meet his client's eyes.

James nodded, then downed half the contents of his glass before answering. "Yah, that leaves my ass swinging in the wind doesn't it? Course, I could try for witness protection. I wonder if they would like to hear how their precious lab is selling organs to the Ukrainian mafia? Hmm?

Or maybe they'd like to hear how the director of that aforementioned lab helped to concoct evidence in the murder of my wife. Of course, he couldn't have done it without help from his pretty little assistant. Oh, sorry, counsellor. You don't even want to get into this kind of conversation, do you?"

Several minutes passed in silence while James stared into the now empty glass, as though trying to find an answer there. Finally he rose, set the glass on the table, and made his way to the door. "Counsellor, it's been a real eye opener."

Dennis Foster lingered over his drink, pondering his best choice of action under the circumstances. He was a good lawyer, and won far more cases than he lost. His reputation was sound, his marriage adequate and his future looked prosperous. If the thin patch in his previously thick head of hair was extending a bit too rapidly, it only contributed to his appearance of maturity among his peers. Yes, life was good, and he was determined to make sure it stayed that way.

What, after all, could Sinclair say about him? He had admitted nothing, even when Sinclair made his veiled accusations. He'd write the visit up as a legal consultation during which he'd taken no retainer. With a sigh, Foster rose from the comfortable embrace of the chair. There was one more detail to be taken care of.

When the phone was answered on the third ring he didn't wait for a greeting. "Malcolm, remember that book I was telling you about?"

"Yeah, I remember."

"I had a chance to finish it last night. Fascinating story. I'd highly recommend it."

"What was so good about it?"

"Well, the guy decided to try for a plea bargain after all. His lawyer recommended against it, but the guy figured he might be able to get witness protection."

"Sounds like something I'd be interested in. How'd it end?"

"Oh, come on, Malcolm. I'm not going to give away the ending. I want you to read it for yourself."

"Well, thanks for the tip. I'll be sure to pick it up in the next couple of days."

As he hung up the phone goosebumps rose on Foster's back. Midway into a shrug to throw off the sensation, a picture of Sinclair's macabre marionette dance rose in his mind. He abandoned the motion and moved to the bar for another drink.

He'd made his report. As far as he was concerned, he was finished with the whole sorry mess.

***

"Damn! you're sure that's what he said?" Ralf Altmann's grip on the phone tightened as he listened to his informant's information.

"Yeah, I'm sure. He said the book was fascinating and that the guy decided to choose a plea bargain. What's this all about anyway?"

"None of your God-damned business! You're paid to answer the phone. Nothing more."

Altmann cursed again as he hung up. He'd have to go with "plan B.' He could just imagine the I-told-you-so look on Juan's face when he heard the news. He had vivid memories of his late afternoon stroll on the Florida beach with the Panamanian during the regional meeting a few weeks earlier.

It had not been a pleasant walk, and his discomfort had been due only in part to the unbearable heat.

Juan had opened the conversation once they'd reached an unoccupied stretch of blazing hot sand. "Rosa's death will leave a vacuum in the prostitution trade in Winnipeg, won't it?"

"Well, I'm sure the bikers will fill the void quick enough. I don't think they'll shed any tears when they hear she's dead."

"But what if their bid for the territory is contested? Let's say by a group with a lot of heavy muscle."

"What are you suggesting? We've never messed with that type of business before. It's not worth the hassle!" Altmann swore silently to himself for not having thought to bring a hat. Beads of sweat formed along his hairline and tracked down the side of his face. He refused to give Juan the satisfaction of wiping it away. The little man seemed to get some perverse enjoyment out of seeing gringos suffer from the heat.

"Think about if a bit, Ralf. I'm not saying we actually make a move for the territory. Just the suggestion may be enough to gain a little leverage from the boys who get their kicks out of wearing studded leather.

"Let's say that we need someone to do us a service. For example, someone to eliminate the problem you created with your bungling. We let the bikers think we want the territory, then we tell them they can have it without any fuss from us if they're willing to get rid of our problem. I've heard they're pretty accomplished at what they do, so I'm confident they would be able to take care of James if he decides to cooperate with the authorities."

Juan stooped to pick up a shell from the sand, then sent it skipping across the surface of the water. Ralf felt a certain satisfaction in the fact that the water was too rough to allow more than one skip before the shell sank from sight.

"If the bikers take care of Sinclair," Juan continued. "We wouldn't have to call in our big guns from the east, and if something goes wrong, it will be the bikers who take the fall. And if they go for it, we've received quite a return for letting them have something we didn't even want in the first place." A soft chuckle escaped his thin lips.

Try as he might, Ralf couldn't find a flaw in the plan. By the time he'd returned to the air-conditioned comfort of his room, he had a whole new respect for Juan.

Ralf drew his thoughts back to the present. Yesterday he had received a phone call with a number and instructions he was to use if he needed help with the Sinclair mess. Well, it looked like he needed it, and he'd have to make the call. But first, he had to contact Laury and tell him to get his butt home. There was the little matter of his assistant to take care of.

CHAPTER TWENTY-SEVEN

Stan sat at the tiny table in Taras Podricki's apartment and contemplated his next move. The coffee in his cup was cold, but he swirled the last dregs and tossed it back. He had to get the photocopies of the shipping bills to Inspector Willis. They would need a search warrant for the lab, and somehow they'd have to keep a lid on the investigation until O'Connor could be picked up. Anel would have to make a statement.

He was so exhausted he couldn't think properly. What he needed was a few hours' sleep.

On the sofa, Sonja stirred and moaned softly. Even in dreams she couldn't escape the sad events of her life. Anel was curled in the large armchair, a blanket thrown over her shoulders. In repose she had a little-girl quality about her. She seemed very fragile.

Sonja stirred again and a wave of conflicting emotions tore at him. Taras' narrow bed at the end of the room beckoned, and he fought the temptation to lie down.

Taras . . . the thought of the old man brought back the events of the previous night, weighing his spirits even more.

He woke to Anel's soft hand on his shoulder. He had fallen asleep at the table. As he rubbed a kink out of his neck, he became aware of harsh sunlight coming through the apartment window.

"What a mess," Anel said as she opened the fridge door to examine the contents.

Did she mean the contents of the fridge, his appearance, or the situation? He decided not to bother asking for clarification; her remark covered all three. The couch was empty and he could hear the sound of the shower in the bathroom next to the kitchen. Sonja was also up.

Anel found orange juice in the fridge, poured three glasses and handed one to Stan. The gaze she levelled at him was calm.

"Now I think it's your turn to give me the whole story."

He nodded. He would be doing a lot of explaining in the next few hours. In a few sentences he sketched Sonja's role in the investigation. "She still thinks I'm Dimitri Bolenko. That's something I need to straighten out this morning." He rubbed a hand over the sandpaper of his unshaven jaw. "Then I'm going to clean up and get back to work." As he finished speaking, Sonja emerged from the bathroom, her wet head wrapped in a thin towel.

Anel smiled at the girl, then turned to Stan. "I'm going to run over to the corner store for some groceries. They might even have a disposable razor." She gathered up her purse and left the apartment. She was giving him time to have his talk with Sonja.

How should be begin? Playing for time, he handed her a glass of juice. "Anel found some orange juice . . ."

She accepted the glass but avoided looking directly at him.

"Sonja . . . please, sit down." She sat, still refusing to meet his gaze. He had hurt her deeply, and at this moment he hated his job and the deceit it

231

required. He reached for her hand but she drew back.

"My real name is Stan Boyko. I'm an RCMP undercover officer. I can't begin to tell you how sorry I am that I allowed you to think I was someone . . ."

The corners of her mouth drew down and began to quiver. Heavy tears fell on her folded hands. "You are secret police. It was all a lie. Just a lie. Who speaks the truth anymore?"

Shame and despair weighed heavily on his shoulders. Would she forgive him for the lies he had told her? He realized just how much he wanted her to understand. How stupid can I be? I think I'm falling in love with her, and I can't even admit it to myself. "No, Sonja. It wasn't all a lie. If you can give me just one more day I promise I'll explain everything to you. Right now I need to get the evidence I found last night into the hands of someone who can take care of it. Please, just give me one more day."

He rose and laid his hand on her shoulder. She tensed, but didn't draw away. As he pulled the door shut behind him, she was still at the table, her hands wrapped around the glass of juice.

***

When Anel returned to the apartment twenty minutes later Stan was gone. Sonja stood at the window, her back rigid. With one hand she ruffled the remaining dampness from her hair. Stan had explained his working relationship with Sonja to her, but he had said nothing of his personal relationship with the Ukrainian girl. Anel's intuition told her there was much more between them than he had been willing to explain.

"Dimit . . . Stan has left," Sonja said. She did not turn around. From the sound of her voice she must have been crying when Anel came in.

"He seems like a good man, Sonja. He had a job to do and he did what he thought was best for the greater good. I'm sure he wouldn't deliberately hurt anyone."

Sonja's shoulders drooped and she rested her forehead against the grimy window pane. "For a little while I was happy."

"Did he say he would come back?"

"He said he would call later. I don't know when. He said we would be safe here, but not to let anyone in. People might want to hurt us." She turned from the window, a silhouette in black against the exterior sunshine. "Why would someone want to hurt us?"

Anel realized Sonja knew very little of what was happening. Should she tell her? Maybe if they talked about it, both might remember a detail that would be important. Stan was right. They knew a lot about the case just from being bystanders. There were people who might want to make sure they didn't tell anyone what they knew. But no one knew where they were. They were safe here in the apartment.

She was really hungry. Neither she nor Sonja had eaten since the night before and it was well past noon. She busied herself making sandwiches from the items she had picked up at the corner store, and Sonja began to relax, seeming more comfortable in her company.

They settled in at the kitchen table. Between bites Sonja said, in heavily accented English, "My clothes are dirty. I can go back to the Sinclair house and get clean clothes, do you think?"

"Absolutely not! We don't know where James Sinclair is or what he's up to. But we could buy you a few things. It's not far to the downtown shopping area. We'd blend into the crowds."

"No. Not possible. I have no money."

"I have money, Sonja. Don't worry about it. We'll just pick up a few things."

"No! I have no money. I have clothes at Sinclair's." Sonja ran a finger back and forth along the edge of the table, and refused to meet Anel's gaze.

It was a matter of pride. The girl had no money and no job. Pressing the matter would build a wall between them, which Anel didn't want to do.

"I tell you what . . ." She stopped and laughed when she saw the quizzical look on Sonja's face. She would have to remember to speak slowly and avoid colloquialisms. "I need fresh clothes too, and we're about the same size. I'm sure we can find something for you at my place. We'll go over and come right back. How do you feel about that?"

Sonja's frown forced Anel to rethink her suggestion. Stan had said to be careful. Did he think she might be a target also? But who knew Stan had evidence on Laury? No one, at least not yet. It should be safe to go to her house.

But before they left, she should explain to Sonja what was happening. If James Sinclair had killed his wife, then Stan was right to be worried

234

about the girl. Sonja might be able to provide evidence against Sinclair.

"Sonja," she began, "we need to talk about what's happening. Then we'll decide what to do about getting some fresh clothes." As she summarized the events of the previous night, she realized Sonja understood English quite well, much better than she could speak it. It made the task a lot easier.

"So Stan believes that James Sinclair killed his wife and framed your Uncle Taras. The director of the lab is in Minneapolis right now. That means everything has to be kept quiet so he doesn't hear about it and stay away." Anel purposely had not mentioned her relationship with Laury. The omission came easily; she realized she was becoming good at keeping secrets.

As she related the story, it struck her that it was well into the afternoon and she had not showed up at work. Quite possibly someone had phoned her at home and would have received no answer. What should she do?

At this point, the only thing the staff might know was that the janitor had experienced a heart attack. They wouldn't even know Taras had died. It was important that the routine at the lab appear as normal as possible, in case Laury phoned. She made a swift decision and called the lab.

Pamela answered the phone.

"Oh, hi Anel. I thought you might be in Minneapolis!" Her tone was not warm, but for once Anel didn't care.

235

"I'm feeling under the weather, Pamela. I'll try to get in tomorrow, but from the way I feel, I doubt it."

"No problem, we'll cover for you."

I bet you will Anel thought, but she thanked Pamela and hung up, hoping she had made the right move.

Now, what to do about the clothes. If they went to her place, she could park behind the townhouse, or even a few blocks down the street. And they could be in and out in a matter of ten minutes.

"Okay, Sonja. It's time you saw a little bit of Winnipeg. I'll give you a guided tour on the way to my place."

They left the apartment and were greeted at the bottom of the stairs by a strange apparition in a wildly patterned dress. The woman stood her ground, a look of determination on her face, both hands planted firmly on broad hips.

"What the hell's going on here anyway? People traipsin' in and out at all hours of the night. It's gettin' so a body can't get a decent night's sleep. Where's Taras? I wanna talk to him."

At the mention of her uncle's name, Sonja's eyes grew bright with tears. "Oh, Miranda. Uncle Taras . . ." She turned her back on the startled neighbour and buried her face in her hands. It was left to Anel to explain that Taras had died of a heart attack during the night.

"Ah, honey," Miranda's voice softened as she addressed Sonja. "That's the shits. Sorry I flew off the handle. You need anything, you just call on Miranda. I'll give you a helpin' hand." A skinny man in a black leather jacket came to the door of

Miranda's apartment and lounged against the frame. It was obvious to Anel that he didn't share any of the group's pain. Miranda didn't bother to introduce him.

"Anythin' I can do for you now, sweetie?" she continued.

Sonja just shook her head, unable to reply.

Anel said, "She just needs some clean clothes. I'll be able to help her out." She put her arm around Sonja and eased her out the front door.

CHAPTER TWENTY-EIGHT

Cobra pulled into the parking lot to get a better look at the car. Yes, a grey 1982 Mercedes 380 SL convertible. Fortune was smiling on him. Word on the street was Road Dawg wanted the car located. How many grey 380 SLs could there be in the city? Not many. He pulled his Harley into the 7-11 across the street from the apartment and punched the number for the clubhouse into his cell phone.

"Yah, this is Cobra. You can tell Road Dawg I found that Mercedes he was lookin' for. It's in the alley behind the Rossburn Arms. It's an apartment house on St. Mary's Road, couple'a blocks down from Rooster's Restaurant."

"Stick with it," the voice said. The line went dead.

Cobra slipped the cell phone into his pocket and circled the block once more. At the head of the alley he pulled into the curb. Just his luck! The car had gained a driver and was backing out. He eased up the street a half block and waited until the Mercedes cleared the alley and merged with northbound traffic. He followed, keeping well back.

They cut over to Dunkirk then onto the St. Vital bridge, then took a left at Jubilee. They were headed for Tuxedo. The phone in Cobra's pocket came to life. "Stick with it,' he'd been told. He ignored the call. Fifteen minutes later they cruised past a mansion with crime-scene tape stretched across the driveway. The Mercedes slowed, and then came to a stop at the curb.

Cobra continued on for a full block, made a right, and pulled over. It must be the Sinclair place. Bet that's Sinclair driving the car! If Road Hawg is lookin' for you, man, you screwed the wrong people.

As he contemplated his next move, his cell rang. He'd ignored two more calls while he'd tracked the car.

"Cobra, here."

"Where the hell are you?" It was Road Hawg, and he wasn't happy.

***

Stan spread the photocopies out on Inspector Willis' desk as he gave him a quick overview of the past twelve hours. "This is the proof we need to nail both their asses to the wall." He stabbed at one pile of paper then another as he spoke. "Here, the delivery to the lab, and here" the delivery to the airport. Very few of the organs delivered to the lab stayed there longer than two hours." He slammed his fist on the desk, then began to pace.

He was tired, he was angry, and he was worried about Sonja and Anel. Not a good combination. Moreover, he was emotionally involved. Of all the people in Winnipeg, why was it Sonja he was attracted too? And Taras . . . his heart attack was brought on by the stress of the past few days.

"Stan, sit down. There's something going on here that I don't understand. Is this case getting to you?" Willis motioned to a chair in front of his desk.

Stan was tempted to sit, but debated whether he'd be able to get up again if he did. In the end, he gripped the chair back for support and looked at

Willis, freshly groomed and composed. It brought home to him how dishevelled he must appear. He raked a hand through his hair, then gave up. What was the use?

He glanced at his superior again and saw compassion in his eyes. Willis was truly concerned. Stan knew his best course of action was to spill his guts and get off the case. But first, he had to know where Sinclair was.

He lowered his exhausted body into the chair and exhaled loudly. His shoulders slumped as his spine relaxed. He met Willis' eyes. "Yeah, I guess it is getting to me. I used a man last night, with no regard for his safety, and I watched him die."

Willis shook his head as he spoke. "There's nothing you did""

"Oh, I know. I didn't cause his death. Not directly, anyway. But I was part of it. And now his niece is out there, and she's linked to Sinclair. Who knows how much danger she's in? No one knows where she is right now, but I'm still kicking myself for leaving her unprotected."

This time Willis nodded. "She's in danger. Where is she? We'll have one of our guys pick her up. Rosa's murder has been classified as an organized crime problem, so it's in our jurisdiction now."

Stan could just imagine Sonja's panic if uniformed police officers showed up at Taras' door and asked her to come with them. But if Anel was there, Sonja might not panic. Before he answered Willis' question, Stan asked one of his own. "Did you get a chance to talk to that junkie yet? What was his name? Walter?"

Again Willis nodded. "We talked to him. I think he was spouting off to get your attention." Willis paused. "But we can't totally disregard what he said. He'd heard some talk about something big going down. A hit that would affect the bikers' territory. The word was, if someone did them a service, a payback might be expected. He couldn't be more specific than that. But, as I said, he might have put his own spin on the conversation just for our benefit."

Stan said, "Something big did go down, but it's hard to say. There might be something behind Walter's story, or it could be a load of bullshit."

Willis grinned. Then he sobered. "Okay, where's this niece? If Taras was framed, Sinclair becomes our prime suspect. And if he thinks the girl can incriminate him, for her own safety, we need to bring her in."

Stan knew it was time he gave Willis the full story. When he did, he'd be removed from the case, but that didn't mean he'd step back and let someone else protect Sonja and Anel. He took a deep breath and began his story.

***

Clutching the steering wheel of the Mercedes with trembling hands, James stared at the crime scene tape barring him from his own driveway. Shit, how had it come to this? The whole goddamned world was coming down around his head.

After leaving the lawyer's office earlier this morning, he'd driven around for a while, his brain in a fog. His aimless wandering eventually put him within a few blocks of the apartment where he kept his most sensitive documents. No one else had entered it since he'd rented it six years earlier.

As he paced the worn carpet, he tossed around a few alternatives, none of which made any sense. Maybe he should get away for a while, give himself a chance to clear his head. He could go to the cottage at Falcon Lake for a few days. No, scrap that idea. Detective Berger had warned him against leaving town. The cops were sure to think he was trying to make a run for it.

His chest felt tight again, and that helped him make his decision. The last thing he wanted was to get himself into some isolated place and then need a doctor. Packing his files into a large box he headed for the door. There was one folder in the house he should get, then he'd drive downtown and turn himself in.

Now, as he contemplated the house he used to call home, he realized he'd have to make do without the file. There was no way he could cross that crime scene tape without being immediately arrested. That was the last thing he needed. He had more than enough material in the trunk to buy his immunity anyway. He put the car in gear, took a final look at his house, and set off down the street. As he rounded the corner he noticed a Harley Davidson at the curb. Turquoise paint job, black saddlebags. A bike just like it had passed him when he pulled over at the house. A premonition of danger raised gooseflesh along his arms.

Stepping on the accelerator, he made a quick right into the alley. If the bike was following him, there was a chance he could confuse the driver long enough to cut back to the street before the biker realized what was going on.

By the time James realized his mistake it was too late. The alley was a long isolated tunnel. High security fences rose on either side of him. Blank walls with locked gates. As he shot down the narrow lane, two bikes turned in at the mouth of the alley, a solid wall of growling machinery. James hit the brakes and slammed the car into reverse. Two bikes coasted to a stop at the other end of the narrow lane. He was trapped.

Do something, his brain screamed. Hit the horn. Dial 911. But his hands refused to obey the commands.

Instead, his grip tightened on the steering wheel. As the machines moved in from either end, James felt his bladder give way. Urine pooled on the leather seat, and he marvelled at the warmth of it. He'd have to have the car detailed again. Who was he kidding? Rosa had died surrounded by satin and lace; he'd die surrounded by piss stained leather and blood spattered glass.

CHAPTER TWENTY-NINE

Anel slowed as she drove past her townhouse. Everything seemed okay. No lurking bogey-men, no strange cars with someone hunched behind the wheel. She drove around the corner and parked well down the street.

"Okay, Sonja," she said to the girl at her side. "I think it's okay to go inside. We'll be very quick. Are you ready?"

Sonja nodded and smiled.

She's really very pretty, Anel realized. No wonder Stan is attracted to her. The thought caused only a momentary sadness, and it died quickly. She felt stripped of emotion" barren. Last evening, Stan's revelations in the lab made it clear that Laury had entangled her in his crooked dealings. Just as she'd begun to let down her guard, she had been used. It wouldn't happen again.

She led Sonja down the alley to the back gate of her tiny yard, lifted the latch and peered around. No one. The townhouse wasn't being watched. Sonja crowded in close behind her as she slipped the key into the lock on the back door and eased it open. The interior of the townhouse was silent.

How ridiculous can this be? It's my home and I feel like a thief! She let her breath out in a sigh of relief and stepped inside.

The phone rang, the sound shrill in the quiet room. Anel's heart leapt in her chest and she suppressed a scream. Sonja grabbed Anel's arm and gasped. Both girls stared first at each other, then at the ringing instrument on the kitchen counter. Finally Anel reached for it.

"Hello," she managed to whisper.

"Well, hello!" It was Laury. "I was beginning to worry about you. I called the lab and they said you'd called in, sick. I phoned earlier but there was no answer."

She cleared her throat and swallowed with difficulty. What should she say? She couldn't let him get suspicious. It didn't take much effort to give her voice a feeble quality. "I'm really not feeling well. I heard the phone ring, but I've been in and out of the bathroom. Maybe something I ate . . . or stomach flu. How's the . . . the convention?"

"Terrible. I'm lonely, and I'd love to have you join me."

"Oh. Sorry, but it's out of the question. I feel so miserable . . . But, I . . . I should be back to work tomorrow" for sure the next day. "She turned to Sonja and mouthed the word "Laury." Sonja's eyes grew large. She backed away, covering her mouth with her hand.

Anel's mind raced. Had someone at the lab mentioned the incident of the janitor to him? Probably not. Who would have brought it to the staff's attention? When Laury spoke again, she detected a hint of tension in his voice.

"It's too bad you're under the weather. Well, I won't keep you. Get back to bed and take care of yourself."

She thanked him and hung up. Disgust flooded her; then she fought the desire to weep. "Come on, Sonja. Let's get some clothes and get out of here."

In her bedroom, Anel grabbed a tote bag and shoved a few pairs of underwear into it. She whipped a pair of cotton pants off a hanger and rolled up two pairs of jeans. Everything went into the bag. Where's my red sweater? And the striped one? If she was going to share clothes with Sonja, she'd need at least two sweaters. Then she remembered having hand washed several items on Saturday. They were in the basement on the drying rack.

She turned to go downstairs, then decided to send Sonja for the sweaters while she finished packing a few things from the bathroom. Just talking to Laury on the phone had increased her unease. She wanted to get out of the house as fast as possible.

"Sonja, downstairs . . ." She used her fingers to indicate walking down a flight of stairs, "Downstairs there are some sweaters drying. Can you bring them up here for me? We'll need them." Did the girl understand?

"Downstairs . . ." Sonja frowned then her brow cleared. "Basement. Yes, in basement you have sweaters. Of course." She headed down the stairs.

In the bathroom Anel scooped her toothbrush and makeup into the side pocket of the tote bag. What else will we need? Oh, right. Some socks. She turned to go back to her bedroom. Laury was leaning against the door frame.

"I see you've recovered. Are you going somewhere?"

***

"Anel? Sonja? Open the door, it's me, Stan." Still no reply. He pounded on the flimsy door with

246

his fist. He was about to put his shoulder to it to force it open when Miranda called from the bottom of the stairs.

"Well, hello Mr. Ukrainian sailor. The girls aren't there. They went out."

"What do you mean, not there? Did you see them leave? Were they with someone?" Shit! I told them to stay put! He made it to the bottom of the stairs in record time.

"Nope. They were alone. Went out 'bout . . . hmmm, 'bout a half hour ago, maybe a bit longer."

"Did they mention where they were going?" Miranda shrugged and shook her head. "Think, Miranda," Stan prompted. "It's very important."

Miranda drew back in surprise. "Hey, what the hell happened to your accent? You a cop, sweety-pie?" She fished in the pocket of her voluminous dress, extracted a pack of cigarettes and parked a hip against the wall. "You got some explainin' to do."

Stan itched to grab the woman by her fleshy shoulders and give her a good shake.

From inside her apartment a man bellowed, "Everything okay out there, Miranda?"

"Yah, yah, settle down," she called over her shoulder then she turned her attention back to Stan. "What the hell's goin' on around here, Mr. Po-leece man? That's what you are, aren't you?"

"Miranda, I don't have time to explain. I can tell you that both those girls are in danger if I don't find them quickly. Can you tell me exactly what they said when they left?"

She fished a book of matches from her pocket and lit a cigarette. As the smoke curled upward she frowned, squinting into the middle distance. Finally, bringing her focus back to Stan she replied. "Seems to me Taras' niece wanted some clean clothes. The other one said she could help her out. Somethin' like that."

"Did they say they were going shopping? It's really important that I know where to find them."

"Nope. Didn't say anything 'bout shopping. She said, "I can help her out.' That's all."

"Help her out . . . help her out." Stan muttered the words to himself. If she was going to take Sonja shopping she probably wouldn't have said "help her out.' No, it sounded more like she was planning to lend her some clothes. It made sense. They were about the same size. Anel had probably taken Sonja to her place. She wouldn't be worried about her safety since Laury was out of town. Still, he didn't like it.

"Miranda, can I use your phone?" She led him into the apartment and pointed to the phone sitting on top a battered phone book. He found Anel's number and dialled. No answer. The girls might not have gone to the house, or they might be on their way back all ready. There was no way of knowing for sure where they were. He scribbled Anel's address on the palm of his hand.

He glanced around but couldn't see the man who had called out to Miranda. That was odd. The apartment wasn't that large. He thanked the woman and left.

Back on the street he paced, then kicked at the front tire of the borrowed car to vent some frustration. What should he do? He couldn't just sit in front of the apartment waiting for them to come back. He had her address, he might as well drive over and check things out.

***

Sonja made her way across the dark basement area, her hands stretched in front of her. Where was the light switch? Maybe she missed it at the top of the stairs. This basement was nothing like the Sinclair's professionally finished lower level with large windows that let in the light.

Something brushed her face and a scream welled in her throat. Her fingers grabbed at it, a piece of string. That made sense: the light was controlled by a pull chain. She snapped the light on and scanned the room. It was a large open area with one small window set high on the wall at either end of the room. Both were covered with dark curtains. The washer and dryer were in a corner, while off to the side stood a collapsible clothes rack, hung with several light-weight sweaters. Pleased with her find, she took them from the rack, snapped off the light, and was plunged into darkness.

After a moment her eyes adjusted and she made out light coming from the top of the stairs through the partially open door. With a sigh of relief, she shuffled across the floor and started up the stairway.

The sound of a struggle came from the other side of the door. She heard voices. A man was speaking rapidly and he sounded angry. Really angry.

". . . did you think you were going to do, Anel? Run to the police and tell them about your own part in this?"

Then she heard Anel.

"Please, Laury. I know nothing about what was happening. Just leave me alone. What are you doing? Let go of me."

Anel sounded terrified, and she called the man Laury. A cold shiver sliced through Sonja and her legs went weak. Somehow, Laury O'Connor had gotten into the house. But he was supposed to be in Minneapolis. How had he gotten back? She lowered herself onto a step before her legs gave way. She had to think.

If Laury and Anel were on the other side of the door that meant they were in the kitchen.

"Stop it, Laury. Leave me alone. What . . . I said let me go!"

"It's too bad this didn't work out, Anel. If you had cooperated a little more, we'd have nothing to worry about. Hold still! We're going for a little ride. There's someone I want you to meet."

Laury didn't know Sonja was in the house. If she surprised him, maybe there was a way she and Anel could get out the back door. Sonja eased the door open a fraction of an inch, but couldn't see them. From their voices, she calculated that they were directly behind the door. Another inch . . . Laury's shoe came into view. He had his back to the door.

Gathering her strength, Sonja shoved the door as hard as she could, using the full weight of her body. The door connected with Laury's back, sending him sprawling with Anel beneath him. He looked winded and disoriented as he tried to get up.

Sonja grabbed Anel's arm to help her to her feet. They needed to get out before Laury recovered. "Come, Anel. Hurry. Please, hurry!"

Laury staggered to his feet and backed away, blocking the exit to the back door. They were trapped. He shook his head like a wounded bear and focused on them. Sonja read hate in his expression. If he could, she was sure he would kill them both. As though he had read her mind, Laury reached into his coat and pulled out a small gun.

Sonja helped Anel stand and kept a firm grip on her hand. Together, they eased toward the door to the living room, but Laury was across the kitchen in two strides and again blocking their exit. The only way for them to go was into the basement, a dead end.

Laury realized he had them trapped; a grin spread across his face. As he smiled, a tiny trickle of blood oozed from the corner of his mouth. Sonja shuddered. When he hit the floor he had either bitten his tongue or banged his teeth. The blood gave his handsome face a sinister look. He ran the back of his hand across his mouth and examined the crimson stain it gathered. His eyes grew dark with fury when he saw the blood.

"I can make a call and have someone come over to help me out, or you can both come with me to someplace where we can talk this over in a civilized manner. What's it going to be?"

Beside her, Anel whimpered and shook her head. Sonja clutched her hand tighter and mustered her courage before shouting, "Get out of here. Now!"

The basement door was open behind them. She wheeled around and pulled Anel with her. Once they cleared the door, she pulled it shut. There was no lock. Together they groped their way to the bottom of the dark stairs.

Laury opened the door and laughed as he called out, "And where do you think that will get you? If I have to go down there after the both of you I'll be really mad. Worse, if I have to call for help, it isn't going to sit well with certain individuals. I'll give you a minute to think about it."

Anel sank to the floor behind the stairs and began to cry softly. Either the fall had disoriented her, or she was emotionally shattered. She would be no help if Laury came down the stairs. Sonja took several deep breaths trying to ease the tremors shaking her body. She couldn't fight back if she lost control.

Her eyes began to adjust to the dark. There must be something they could use as a weapon. She'd just have to find it. Boxes took up most of the space behind the stairs; an old wooden stand held a record turntable, and a fake Christmas tree was collapsed against a wall. Moving cautiously, she made her way to the back wall where a long counter ran along its width. Her spirits rose. Maybe it was a workbench where she could find some tools. A hammer would make a very good weapon. Unfortunately, except for a layer of dust, the counter was bare.

As she turned to make her way back to Anel, Sonja spotted a dark object leaning against the end of the counter. It was a four-foot length of board. If she swung it hard enough as Laury came around the end of the stairs, she could inflict a bit of damage, even knock the gun from his hand.

"All right, girls. Have you come to your senses?" Laury called. His tone was harsh. Anel curled into a ball and placed her hands over her ears. Sonja gripped the board harder and prayed-Hospody pomozhy menee.

He came down a few steps, stopped, then muttered, "Stupid bitches."

His shoes and pant cuffs were visible on the stairs; there was no back to the stair risers. Sonja eased the board up, carefully positioning it behind the next stair tread.

"I'm not very happy with you girls. You're forcing my hand and that pisses me off." Laury's foot came down to rest on the next tread, Sonja took a deep breath and shoved the board with all her strength between the risers.

It connected with Laury's heel shoving his foot off the stair. He yelled as he lost his balance and tumbled down the stairs. At the bottom, his head smacked hard on the concrete floor and the gun fell from his hand.

Sonja darted out from behind the stairs to make sure Laury was down for good. As she moved toward his still body, a bellow of rage stopped her. The figure of a man stood silhouetted against the light at the head of the stairs.

She moved quickly to reach the gun, but he was faster. The wooden staircase shook as he plunged down the stairs and grabbed her tightly against him. It was only then that she realized it was Stan.

Her adrenalin died, and she broke into sobs. She had killed a man. The sound of his head hitting the hard floor was still in her mind. She sagged against Stan as he kissed her hair, her neck, her cheek. He murmured soft "shhhs" as he stroked her back. "You're okay, you're okay," he whispered again and again.

A scream cut through the basement and a shot rang out. The sounds vibrated off the concrete walls and blended as they hung in the air.

Stan grunted in pain and spun away from her, clenching his side. A whir of motion came from behind the stairs and Anel emerged clutching the board. Laury was propped on one elbow at the foot of the stairs, his back to her, the gun swinging in her direction. Anel slammed the board into the back of his head. Laury collapsed on the floor, the gun falling from his hand.

CHAPTER THIRTY

Stan shifted on the narrow bed. The motion sent a bolt of pain across his mid-section. A curse slipped from between his clenched teeth. "Shit!"

Rudy Savage chuckled from his position at the far end of the bed, "Now, now, Stan. Not in the presence of a lady, and everyone else in this hallway."

Stan drew his eyebrows together in a frown. He still found it hard to concentrate, but his mind was becoming clearer. The anaesthetic must be wearing off. Looking around, he realized he was in a partitioned alcove at the end of a hospital hallway.

For a while he'd been vaguely aware of dozens of people parading past his bed. Glancing to his right, he saw Sonja standing there. Sonja. Thank God she was okay. Where was Anel? Then he remembered. The basement in Anel's townhouse . . . passing out . . . waking up in the ambulance . . . The paramedics had shaken their heads when he'd asked about Laury but they wouldn't tell him more. Then he'd lost consciousness for the second time.

"Anel." The word came out more as a croak than a word, but Sonja understood.

"I think she is okay." Tears came to her eyes, but a smile lit her face. "You are lucky you are alive."

Rudy moved forward. "You were in the operating room for about an hour, Stan. You're one lucky son-of-a"" He caught himself. "Son-of-a-gun. The bullet missed your liver and your kidneys. The doc says it'll take a while to heal, and you'll have quite the scar to remind you of your little adventure."

"And Laury? What happened to Laury?" I blew it! I should have checked to make sure he was out of commission before I went to Sonja. It was hard to think. His head felt thick with fuzzy half-formed thoughts and questions.

Ken McFairlain approached the alcove as Stan asked his question. "He didn't make it. He saved the taxpayers the cost of a trial." Ken grinned as he took in the sight of Stan hooked up to several portable machines. "Bet you never thought you'd experience a taste of hallway medicine. How long are you going to be stuck out here before they find you a room?"

Sonja smoothed the covers over his chest and patted them for good measure. "Tomorrow they have room for you, Stan."

"Tomorrow!" Stan muttered. His mouth was dry. "I'll be out of this hospital tonight if I have anything to say about it."

"You have nothing to say about it," Ken interrupted. "You're an RCMP officer and you've been ordered to stay put until the doctors say you're ready to leave. Hospital room, or no hospital room." His smile erased any harshness that might have accompanied the words.

Stan rolled his head on the inadequate pillow and groaned. He was outnumbered, and he knew it. He gathered Sonja's hand in his own and gave it a gentle squeeze. "How are you doing, Sonja? Okay?"

She nodded. When she spoke it was almost a whisper. "I thought I killed the man. But it . . . Anel she . . ." She turned to Ken. "Anel, she is okay?"

Ken nodded. "She's shook up, but I think she'll be okay. I left her with Berger, of Major Crimes division. As a matter of fact, she sent along a message for Stan." He paused for dramatic effect, then continued. "She said: "Tell Stan to give her a kiss for me.'"

Stan glanced at Sonja, who coloured slightly but grinned.

Ken cleared his throat and backed away from the bed. "I think I'll be running along. Keep us informed . . ."

"Oh, no, you don't," Stan protested. His voice cracked and once again he licked his dry lips. "I want a few details. I know the shit hit the fan on this case. Start talking."

The light atmosphere died. Sonja scooped a spoonful of ice chips from a bucket on a tray and placed them in his mouth. The small amount of water from the melting chips was like nectar to his parched throat.

"You chose a pretty apt expression, Stan," Rudy said. "The shit did hit the fan, and it'll be flying for a couple of weeks. A concerned citizen in Tuxedo reported what they thought were gunshots in an alley. When the police arrived, they found Sinclair dead, in his Mercedes. Someone wanted him silenced, but whoever it was didn't know about the surprise package in the trunk."

Stan cocked an eyebrow in silent question. Ken took up the story.

"Wherever Sinclair was off to, he was taking his files with him. Every last one of them. There's enough in those boxes to put a lot of people away for a long time. It wasn't only Laury O'Connor who was in on the lab shenanigans. Winnipeg's going to lose a couple of other businessmen, including some doctors, to our justice system."

Stan nodded. The movement caused his head to swim. "Any idea how O'Connor got back to Winnipeg? Someone had to have tipped him off. He wasn't supposed to be in town for another couple of days."

Ken shrugged. "We might never know the answer to that one. It's a good thing Sonja was with Anel when Laury found her. If it hadn't been for this little lady's quick thinking . . ." The words were left unsaid, the meaning clear.

"By the way, Sonja," Rudy said, "I caught someone in your uncle's apartment. When Stan was taken off the case, Inspector Willis sent me over there to make sure you were safe. I guess I just missed Stan when he went looking for you. Anyway, when I got to the apartment, Taras' landlady and some punk were ransacking the place. Any idea what they were looking for?"

Sonja nodded and laced her fingers together so tightly the tips went white. She chewed her lower lip for a moment and then spoke. "I think it was for eggs. Uncle Taras spoke of this treasure to Miranda. Miranda might have told the man."

"Eggs?" Stan asked. His mouth dropped open. "Eggs?" Then he remembered. Taras said something about eggs when he had his heart attack. "Help

Sonja . . . eggs must go back . . . the money . . ." But it made no sense.

Sonja drew a deep breath, then relaxed as she blew it out. "He stole World War II treasure, Faberge eggs. He said I must be the one to give them back. He was very ashamed of what he did. I will be happy to give back. These eggs, they caused enough pain."

Rudy gave a low whistle. "Faberge eggs! Wow. They would be worth a fortune. And you'll get a hefty reward. I've read of other cases where stolen art objects were returned. Lloyds of London is still paying out insurance money on them. You'll have no problem looking after yourself for the next couple of years."

Sonja nodded, but there was a look of abject misery on her face. Rudy and Ken shuffled their feet and fidgeted, obviously uncomfortable in the presence of her despair. Stan braved a stab of pain and raised his hand to touch her cheek. "What is it, Sonja? What's the matter?"

"It's just . . . just that I now have to go back to Ukraine. I want to stay here."

Stan felt a warm wave of contentment steal over him. Maybe it was the anaesthetic? Her hand in his? There was more than one way to ensure she stayed in Winnipeg. He'd start working on it. He felt his body relax and he went with the feeling. As he started to drift off, he heard Rudy and Ken reassuring her something could be done.

Then from very far away he heard, "Hey, Stan. I hear you asked Willis for a transfer to a desk job. Have you finally had enough of being . . ."

EPILOGUE

Anel smiled her thanks to Michael Berger as he handed her the drink. He looked flushed, although it wasn't overly warm in the banquet hall, and she noticed that somewhere in his trip between their table and the bar he had removed his coat and tie.

She had spent a lot of time with the police officer in the months following the investigation, and had come to appreciate his keen mind and caring nature. To her surprise, she found she could relax in his company. No, more than relax, she enjoyed his company.

"Are you feeling okay, Michael?" She followed the direction of his gaze and realized he was watching Rudy and Ken, looking quite respectable in their tuxedos, at one end of the bar. The two men grinned broadly and raised their glasses, as though to toast her. She understood then that she and Michael were the objects of some friendly speculation. I don't mind. I truly don't mind. It even feels good. She smiled back, acknowledging their gesture with a nod.

"I see the men are being boys tonight," she quipped. Michael flushed again and cleared his throat. She had been told that while on the job he was all business, direct or even abrupt. With her though, he was as soft as a teddy bear. The first strains of music saved him from having to reply.

They watched Sonja and Stan stepped onto the dance floor. Stan drew Sonja into his arms and they began their first dance as a married couple. They were perfect together, their bodies moving in a graceful unison that was pure joy to watch.

A peaceful feeling crept over Anel and she closed her eyes to savour it. A year ago she had given up all hope she would ever feel this content. The therapy arranged by Victim's Services had helped: she could now live with the realization that she had been abused as a child, and that she had killed a man. But she knew that in large part, she could thank this gentle giant sitting beside her for the healing she had experienced.

When she opened her eyes again he was looking at her. His gaze was soft, filled with warmth and caring.

"Have you given any thought to the offer Victim's Services made you last week?" he asked.

She nodded. She had given it a lot of thought. Could she do it? Could she work with battered and abused women? Women who had been taken advantage of? Used and set adrift, much as she and Sonja were? Could she show them there was hope, no matter how hard the circumstances might have been? Sonja herself was proof of that. Could she be the same?

As though he read her mind, Michael said, "You'd do a great job, Anel." It was a simple statement, but it persuaded her. Offering his hand Michael asked her to dance. When she put her hand in his, it fit perfectly.

THE END